HER VIKEN MATES

INTERSTELLAR BRIDES® PROGRAM: BOOK 11

GRACE GOODWIN

GET A FREE BOOK!

JOIN MY MAILING LIST TO BE THE FIRST TO KNOW OF NEW RELEASES, FREE BOOKS, SPECIAL PRICES AND OTHER AUTHOR GIVEAWAYS.

http://freescifiromance.com

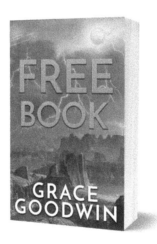

INTERSTELLAR BRIDES® PROGRAM

YOUR mate is out there. Take the test today and discover your perfect match. Are you ready for a sexy alien mate (or two)?

VOLUNTEER NOW!

interstellarbridesprogram.com

1

*R*ager, *Planet Viken, Northern Array, Medical Bay 1*

MY EYES WERE CLOSED AS I RELISHED THE MOMENT, bombarded by my other senses. Soft, silky skin under my hands. The hard pulse of my own heartbeat raging through my cock like pain-filled thunder. The soft scent of feminine heat surrounded me, the musky aroma of my mate's hot, wet pussy just inches away from my eager mouth and I drew in a deep breath, savoring her desire, the mindless anticipation of her body as I made her wait for what only I could give her.

She was *mine*. Her thighs quivered beneath my large palms, and her whimper of need floated in the air and echoed in my body like a cymbal strike, the reverberations traveling straight to my rock-hard cock in agonizing waves. I welcomed the sweet agony of wanting her so badly. This need, my desire for her was like a drug, ruthless and intoxicating. I never wanted this feeling to end. I'd waited so long for her. My mate.

In some deep, dark corner of my mind I knew this wasn't real. I knew I was unconscious in an examination chair on Viken. My hands were strapped to the firm armrests, not holding her pussy open to taste, lick and suck—and eventually, fuck. I knew the luscious curves and welcoming heat of the woman's body, her desire, her trust wasn't really mine, that I would wake up bereft and alone.

Always alone.

But I didn't care. I couldn't stop, didn't want to stop because it was just so damn incredible. I was sharing the thoughts and desires of another warrior, one who'd already been matched and mated, and this woman was his. Her body was his to master, to conquer, to torment with endless pleasure.

Mine.

No, not mine, but the drive to find the one who did belong to me was driving me on. The idea was more instinct than thought, and I allowed this other warrior's need to guide me because in this moment, I wanted to taste this female, to bring her pleasure, to hear her scream my name.

I opened my eyes to stare with wonder at the woman before me. She was strapped to a table. Thick leather bands around her shoulders, waist and hips ensured she could not escape. Her wrists were secured above her head and her legs, gods help me, her legs were bent and pulled wide, leather straps around her thighs and ankles holding her open, exposing her pussy for my pleasure.

From my position kneeling between her legs, I could not

see her face, but that was a small thing when such a feast lay spread before me. Large breasts heaved as she fought for breath. Hard nipples pointed upward, quivering as she gasped her own need. Her legs trembled, her entire body strung so tightly the slightest touch of my fingertips or a whisper of air on her folds caused her entire body to shift. Her pussy was wet and glistening, the outer lips plump and swollen, bright, hot pink and in my mind I knew she'd just come all over my tongue. I could still taste her wild desire.

She was falling apart, her head thrashing from side to side as I lowered my own and blew a warm flow of air over her tender flesh. Gods, I loved pussy. I loved the complex way a woman found pleasure. Nothing aroused me more than working her body and watching her come apart. Discovering exactly what she liked, where to touch, to stroke, lick.

A pussy was like a musical instrument, pluck and play it the right way and a woman made such beautiful sounds, like the soft whimper that just escaped this female's lips.

She jerked, her pussy muscles opening and clenching as I watched, fascinated. Obsessive. Possessive. She wanted a cock inside her, opening her, filling her. Taking her.

In this dream, this pussy was mine. Only my tongue, my cock, my fingers would fill it.

"Please." Her voice washed over me, through me, and a growl erupted from my throat. I'd been waiting. Waiting for her to beg.

With a grin, I slipped two fingers inside her sheath. The first I used to stroke circles around the deep, hard opening of her womb. She moaned, shifting to get closer, but couldn't with her bindings. I curved the second finger, searched for the secret spot inside her core that I knew would bring her the most pleasure.

She tried to escape, for I knew it was almost too much, the feelings I was wringing from her body. Her back arched off the padded table, but the straps held her in place and I froze. The feelings would be intense, perhaps too much so. I did not wish to scare her. Just the opposite. I could spend hours between her parted thighs, making her feel so good. "Do you want me to stop, mate?"

"No," she breathed. "Please, don't stop."

"Who do you belong to?" I already knew the answer, but the basic animal inside me wanted to hear her say it again. And again. "Tell me who you belong to, and I'll lick your sweet pussy until you scream."

"You." Her pussy clenched around my fingers with her words and my cock jerked painfully in response. Soon, I would bury myself in her wet heat and pump into her until she couldn't take any more pleasure. I would fill her with my seed, the connection made by my seed power would drive her mad with desire, make her scream and writhe and come over and over. I would fill her, fuck her, make her come until she collapsed with exhaustion. Until she knew who she belonged to. Until the only name she remembered was mine.

"Mine." I made sure she heard me as I lowered my lips to her clit—swollen and uncovered from the little hood of flesh—and sucked it into my mouth, flicking it with my tongue. Her taste exploded in my mouth and I groaned at the exquisite flavor of her sweet nectar. Sweet, spicy. Perfect. This was mine. All for me.

Working her with tongue and fingers, I brought her to

the peak and stopped. Waited. Sucked and licked again. Harder. Faster.

When she was about to come, I slowed my pace and pulled my fingers from her, leaving her empty and aching. Desperate.

"Please!" She tried to move, but the restraints held her open to me. Her muscles quivered and shook. She could not resist. Could not escape.

My cock was eager. I looked down to discover I was already naked, a drop of pre-cum gathered on the tip of my hard length.

With a grin, I gathered the liquid and stood.

"Are you ready, mate?"

"Yes! Gods, hurry. Fuck me. Do it!"

I chuckled. So eager, my little mate.

With her rich essence lingering on my tongue, I pushed forward in one smooth thrust, filling her with my cock as she moaned, her pussy muscles clamping down on me like a hot fist.

But that wasn't enough. I needed her to come all over my hard cock. I wanted to feel her pussy spasm, out of control as her pleasure took her. To feel her juices coat me as she took me deeper, milked me of my seed.

Buried deep, I lifted my finger and rubbed the drop of pre-cum all over her perfect little clit and watched. Waited.

Seconds later she screamed. The walls of her pussy rippled and pulsed as an orgasm rolled through her. Her nipples were hard, erect little tips and I pulled them gently, rolling them between my fingers as I jerked my hips, pushing harder, deeper as her body exploded around me.

Mine. She was mine. Only I could do this to her. Only I could bring her such pleasure.

With a roar of my own I pumped into her, drawing out her orgasm as more pre-cum coated the inside of her pussy, driving her to the edge again, binding her to me, making her mine.

My body responded to hers as if she were the one with all the power. I thrust into her, nearly mindless, the taste of her heightening my instinct to conquer, claim. Fill her with my seed. My child inside her. My cum. My mate.

Fire built in my blood, centered in my balls as tension built, then exploded. I bellowed as I filled her with my seed, marking her like an animal.

I felt like an animal. Mindless. Wild. Out of control.

Only she could do this to me. And I wanted more. Needed more. Only she made me feel whole.

Pain and pleasure. Lust and love. Obsession and protection. A dozen emotions warred within my body as I filled her, claimed her.

I lowered my lips to her sweat-damp body, to kiss and explore. To ease and worship. I wanted to taste her skin. Nuzzle her. Comfort her. I needed to be gentle now as badly as I'd needed to be wild moments ago.

The urge was nearly painful, my heart squeezing in my chest, pain gathering behind my eyes like hot daggers that burned.

Her skin was so close. Inches away. I was inches away from paradise...

"Rager?"

The voice was hard and cold, a man's voice. Not what I wanted to hear. I wanted her. Her skin. Her scent. Her touch...

"By the gods, Rager. I knew you were going to be a pain in the ass."

Something sharp stabbed me in the neck and the woman faded instantly from my vision. I hissed at the bite of pain, opened my eyes to see who dared bother me. With a clarity all the more cruel for its contrast to what I'd just experienced, I found myself strapped to a cold, hard exam table in the medical center. The sharp, bitter taste of whatever medication had just been injected into my bloodstream flooded my mouth.

With that taste came memory. Reality.

"Damn it, Doctor. That's disgusting." I was angry, furious. The foreign taste of chemicals drove the lingering flavor of sweet pussy from my mind completely. No matter how hard I tried, I couldn't get her honeyed nectar back on my tongue.

I heard a door open and two sets of heavy boots entered the room.

I knew without looking those boots belonged to Evon and Liam. My friends and brothers-in-arms. The fools who'd talked me into this. The damn chair. The dream.

The doctor slapped me on the arm like we were old friends, pushed a button to retract the restraints and walked away. "Welcome back, Rager."

I rolled my head around on my neck as the manacles were removed from my arms and ankles, stretching, trying to regain some sense of control when all I could think about was pussy. Hot. Wet. Heaven both on my tongue and around my cock. "I didn't want to come back."

The doctor chuckled. "No one ever does."

I sat up as Evon and Liam both came to a stop a few feet in front of me. Loomed over me so I had to look up. I was bigger than both of them, but the testing chair made me feel small, made me feel fucking vulnerable.

"Well?" Evon asked. His family had served the Coalition Fleet for generations. Even now, he and his sister Thalia both served the IQC here in the north. Evon's black uniform and short blond hair indicated his allegiance to Sector 2. But the red band around his biceps, around all of our arms, meant we were Royal Guard. We belonged to all of Viken now, not just our home sectors. And like other warriors on our planet who'd fought the Hive and returned, we were beyond Sector politics now. These two were my most trusted allies. We'd fought the Hive together and survived. Returned whole. They were tough as nails, hardcore killers. And they were both lovesick fools.

"By the gods, I want to punch you right now," I grumbled as I wiped a hand over my face. Fuck, it had been so real. Her skin. The soft sounds of her surrender.

By the gods, perhaps I was as big a fool as these two.

I glanced down at the front of my steel-gray uniform, relieved that no wet spot there revealed the depths of pleasure I'd just experienced, and would be denied forever. I'd come in the dream, but no seed coated my pants like a teenager and his first wet dream. I had no idea how it was possible, but I was glad I wasn't humiliating myself in front of the doctor and my friends. Had they had a similar experience when they were processed for the Interstellar Bride Program? We'd been told it would be mild, a hazy experience that we might not even remember.

So why did I clench my fist to lock the softness of soft skin to me? Had it affected Liam and Evon so intensely? Or was I simply a freak for wanting a mate so badly I was willing to break with centuries of tradition and follow the new order of three warriors sharing a bride, as our kings did. Evon argued that we would have a much higher chance of finding a mate together. Perhaps he was correct. But we were different, we three. And I could not imagine a mate who could accept all of us. It was little more than a child's dream.

A mate? The possessive joy that a warrior had felt when he looked on his woman, conquered her, fucked her? That would never be mine. And now I knew exactly what I was missing. "You're an asshole, Evon. I never should have agreed to this."

I expected the doctor to leave the room, but he seemed occupied at the control panel, so all three of us ignored him as Evon responded. "Why?"

I looked from his pale blue, ice-like eyes to Liam's dark blue gaze and shook my head. "This is never going to fucking work. No woman is going to be matched to all three of us."

It was simply impossible. Liam was from Sector 1, where women were claimed in public. Sector 1 males were obsessed with public fucking and conquering and pleasuring a woman by taking her in the ass in front of everyone. In their sector, that kind of claiming was the ultimate show of submission by their women. A gift given to a worthy warrior. A gift only given through the deepest trust, the most pure consent. Love.

And then there was Evon, who always had to be in command. His sector demanded total submission from a woman, albeit in private. Bondage. Surrender. The warriors there lived for complete and total control. Evon would want a female who would submit, trust him absolutely and yield to his every desire. To place her power, her life and her pleasure into his hands and rely on him to care for her in every possible way.

Me? I cared not about any of those needs. Like most warriors from Sector 3, I simply wanted to feast on a woman's sweet pussy before I filled her with my seed. I wanted to see her full lips wrapped around my cock as she loved me with her tongue, gifted me, allowed me to fuck her mouth just as I loved to have my fill of the honeyed nectar of her feminine heat. I was patient, could take hours working a woman's body with my mouth, linger over her delectable scent, drive her to mindless ecstasy with my tongue over and over before I fucked her and made her mine.

"It worked for the kings." Evon's cold, analytical tone was one I'd heard many times, usually when we were prepping for battle. And this felt like that. The stakes were high. A matched mate? An end to our lonely existence? High stakes, indeed.

"We're not kings. We're not at Viken United. We're stuck in this ice-covered nightmare of a work station. What fucking female is going to want to come here?" Liam walked to my side and leaned his hips against the exam table, facing the doctor. He crossed his arms. "Rager's right, Evon. This was a foolish hope."

Yes, he was correct. The Northern Station was surrounded by icy tundra for hundreds of miles. But the planet relied on the communication station to relay transport and messages from the Coalition Fleet and other member planets. The technical name was Interstellar Quantum Communications array, or the IQC. We were Royal guard, IQC officers, and this station was Viken's link to the rest of the universe. Without it, we'd be stranded in a sea of black space with no way to contact the others, no way to send our warriors to battle the Hive, nor receive brides. No transport. No comms. Nothing but empty, blank space.

We could survive, in theory. The planet would provide, that wasn't a concern, for we'd survived for a millennia before the Hive menace rose to unite the planets behind the warriors of Prillon Prime. It was the Prillon warriors who'd first faced the Hive and they'd fought the longest. The Hive was a menace and the IQC array, our comms and transport capabilities, were crucial to keeping the planet free of them.

What we did here was important, and every warrior assigned to the IQC had been chosen because we knew exactly what was at stake. We had all fought in the war, seen the Hive and their horrors with our own eyes. But hearing Liam agree with me didn't improve my mood. Apparently, it didn't improve Evon's either.

"When I'm right, I'm going to make you both beg me to touch her." The heated desire in Evon's eyes made me grin.

"Is that supposed to be a threat, Evon? Because you're such a controlling fuck, I figured that was how it would be anyway." I laughed then, because Liam chuckled at my declaration, and he rarely laughed at all.

"He's right, you know." Liam's chuckle faded to a grin, but his eyes remained all too serious. And there, in that stormy gaze, was Liam's soul on display. Evon was the strategist, but Liam was the realist. He'd lost his family, grown up hard, the son of a VSS leader. The damn VSS. Our own internal enemy. Worse than the Hive, in a way, since they were Vikens—traitors—who wanted to see a return to civil war, to separate nations now united by the three kings. They'd already tried to assassinate the heir, the Princess Allayna, and return Viken to chaos.

Liam's father was a leader of the Viken Sector

Separatists, one of the men behind the attack on the new princess. By then, Liam was already long gone for the VSS influence. When Liam landed in prison as a teen, and then volunteered to serve in the Coalition Fleet battling the Hive, his family disowned him. He had no blood left, for even his mother hadn't spoken to him in years. And in Sector 1, family was everything. We were his family now. His only family.

Liam lifted his hand to rest on Evon's shoulder. "We know you, Evon. You get one look at a mate and you'll start barking orders like we're back on Noerzen 5 facing down Hive berserkers."

That battle had almost killed us all, but Evon had held the team together. We'd fought like Atlan beasts because he ordered us to, because he led the charge, and we'd survived.

"I will adapt. We'll all adapt." Evon's argument was weak, and we all knew it. I grunted in disagreement as Liam spoke.

"No. We won't." Liam shook his head and his long hair swung in a dark curtain past his shoulders, hiding the rest of his expression from me. But I could hear the desire in his voice, and the despair. "We're too different, brother. If you really want a mate, you will have to find warriors more like you. Hell, we all have different needs. My cock gets hard thinking about my mate's upturned ass, watching as it's stretched open as I slide into her, one sweet inch at a time. I like to see my handprint turn pink on her pert ass cheeks."

Liam elbowed me in the ribs, I assumed to encourage me to second his opinion, but I ignored him. I was half a head taller than both of them, and much larger. They had called me the Bronze Beast in our unit because of both my dark bronze hair color and my size. I was big for a Viken, and impulsive. Sometimes I felt out of control, like a beast in

Mating Fever. Massive warrior loaded with weapons and a bad attitude? Not exactly a good combination. I'd gotten in a lot of trouble when I was younger, a fresh recruit. Now, I counted on Liam and Evon to rein me in and keep me in line. On the rare occasions when I was pushed too far, when I lost my head, one of them was always there to step between me and trouble.

"Why are you elbowing me? I know what gets you off. While a willing ass isn't something I would walk away from, I have simpler tastes."

Evon laughed, slapped my shoulder. "Exactly. Tastes. You'll eat pussy for breakfast, lunch and dinner."

I couldn't help but grin. "Damn right." I thought of the dream, of the female who'd come from my mouth, then my cock. Shit. She'd been bound, but I wouldn't need my mate bound for her to part her thighs, not unless Evon pleasured her first. I was getting hard again and had to adjust myself in my uniform pants. "You'll have her tied to a bed, at your mercy."

Evon shook his head. "She'll give me her trust. The greatest gift."

"It'll never work," Liam grumbled. "A matched mate for one of us is bound to be a little wild. But meet the needs of all three of us? Impossible."

I stood and sighed. We'd done the tests. I was the last of the three of us. Now we waited. And waited, because there was no way on Viken, or any other planet in the universe, that there was a female that loved to be fucked and sucked, controlled and commanded, bent over and completely claimed in public. Nor one who could put up with my impulsive nature, or Liam's dark, brooding silences, or Evon's need to be in control, command every detail of every moment, every encounter. He was relentless, the sun burning in a desert. He never stopped. Never rested.

Even if a female could satisfy us sexually, it would require a truly miraculous event to find a woman who could accept us as men, as true mates. No female could love all of us. To hope was a mistake. I realized that now.

"Then let's get back to work," I said. I wanted to go back to my quarters and take my hard cock in hand, get rid of this excess tension. I needed the dream wrung from my system, but that wasn't going to happen. We had work to do.

"Yeah, we might have been tested, but a match? Fucking impossible. I should have told you two to find another third. I will ruin the chances for both of you." Hearing those words from Evon made me depressed. Since he liked control, perhaps he was the most eager for the match. It was a logical step for a male his age. Mate. Procreate. Neat and tidy. It wasn't so simple up North and it wasn't so simple for Vikens who were attempting to mate as a trio. But Liam and I were also his age. Yes, we wanted a mate as well, one that all three of us would share, who would be perfect for us based on the Interstellar Brides Program matching, but we weren't as jaded. Were we? The testing dream was fading, and so was the dream of a true match.

"Fuck," I muttered.

"Impossible?" the doctor asked. "It seems not." We'd all but forgotten about him. He turned to face us, excitement in his eyes. "No female in the universe to meet your every sexual need? Wrong. There is one." He looked to Liam. "One willing to display her acceptance of what a Sector 1 mate can give." Next he looked to Evon. "A woman willing to surrender control only those from Sector 2 demand." Then he glanced my way. "Content to lie back and enjoy your brand of attention, Rager, from Sector 3."

My heart skipped a beat even as my mind struggled to keep up with what he said. "Doctor?" I was shocked to discover my hands now shook.

He smiled. "Congratulations, warriors. You've been matched."

2

*I*sabella Martinez, Planet Viken, IQC Array, Transport Center

WARDEN EGARA HAD SAID IT WOULD SEEM LIKE A NAP, THE whole transporting across the universe thing. She asked me if I'd had my wisdom teeth pulled and I'd said yes. When I was fifteen, they'd put me to sleep and I'd woken up with gauze wedged in my cheeks, no memory of the two hours it took them to hack out my impacted molars. Thank god.

As I blinked now, I recalled that conversation and tried to figure out where I was. There was no weird, loopy drug in my system. No oral surgeon leaning over me with a light on his head, or the taste of blood in my mouth.

No. When I blinked my eyes open after being transported from the Miami Interstellar Brides Processing Center to Viken, I saw three large men all watching me with an intense interest that made me squirm.

Aliens. They were aliens.

And I was in a land far, far away from Earth.

They had to be aliens, or I really had been given some good drugs, because these three? They were hot. Like, ultra-smoking hot. Magazine-cover-supermodel-combined-with-lumberjack hot. And big, so big they towered over me, despite the fact that they were squatting down around me. Instead of lying in a dentist's chair, I was sprawled out on the floor. I pushed up off the hard, unforgiving surface and they moved quickly, putting their hands on me to help me sit up.

I flinched at the unexpected contact, completely overwhelmed. They were so close. So intense. For a second, I felt like a bug under a microscope. First time in my life I'd ever felt sorry for an insect.

I glanced down, afraid I was covered in blood, or worse, naked. But I breathed a sigh of relief when I saw a modestly cut, flowing white gown covered me from neck to ankle. It clung to my curves like a second skin, sexy and innocent at the same time.

Looking down at the gorgeous dress for courage, I took a deep breath and lifted my gaze. Playing coy, or acting shy would do me no good. Not here. I'd just been transported halfway across the universe to marry and sleep with, say "I do, forever and ever" to a complete stranger, a man I'd never met. And Warden Egara had said something odd about my *mates*. As in more than one. But I'd just blinked and assumed I was hearing things.

So, perhaps I had been drugged after all because these three men were eyeing me as if I were their favorite candy and they each wanted to give me a lick. The idea made me lick *my* lips, which made their eyes drop to my mouth. One of them, I swear, made a rumbly sound in his chest. Their hands were on me, gently touching me as if I couldn't sit up on my own, and the heat of their palms made me shudder as desire rose like a storm inside me. My whole life that darkness had tormented me, making me want what I couldn't have. But that was my old life, right? I'd read the Interstellar Brides Program brochure, and it said their match rate was higher than 98%.

But then, I'd always excelled at being the exception to the rule. The only one of my friends in grade school who *didn't* have a crush on Tommy Parker. The only eighth grade girl in math club. The only woman programmer at a fast-moving Silicon Valley startup until the asshole attitudes of the men in the office drove me to do something I still couldn't quite regret.

Sure, I'd gone to jail for it, but then, I'd ended up here, with three of the hottest men I'd ever seen looking at me like I was dessert. No, not just dessert, chocolate molten cake with a hot fudge center, caramel drizzle and a scoop of creamy vanilla ice cream on the side.

Ultimate dessert.

But I couldn't think with them touching me. Or maybe it was the trip through some kind of dark matter, sub-space, freakish transporter straight out of a *Star Trek* episode. I tried to stand, but the room spun and I plopped right back down before I'd moved more than a couple inches.

"She's hurt." The blond spoke.

"Why is the doctor not here?" That one had dark hair, impossibly black, and it was almost as long as mine.

"I will find him." The one with the wavy, copper-colored hair stood, and holy fuck, he was tall. Like a giant. I tilted my head back and looked up at him as he began yelling at the men who stood behind a control panel of some kind. It was like I just stepped onto the set of a crazy sci-fi movie...with huge, hot aliens. Except, they *looked* human. One head, two eyes, broad shoulders, lean hips, muscles everywhere. Their skin wasn't blue or covered in scales and there were no tentacles in sight. They looked *better* than human, if my libido had a vote.

"I'm fine," I said. I cleared my dry throat and tried again. "Really." I wasn't lying. The room had stopped spinning and the fog in my mind was quickly being overcome with nerves. Was one of these men my match? I was too nervous to ask, but god, I didn't even want to think about it. Not really. They were all amazing, and I didn't want to have to choose.

The giant spun on his heel at my voice and looked down at me, then crouched, an intentional move so he was closer to my level.

"I am Rager, one of your mates."

He wasn't speaking English, but I understood him. Strange. Oh yeah. I touched my fingers to the bump on my temple above my ear. Warden Egara mentioned I would be prepared for transport, including receiving an NPU, a Neural Processing Unit. She said it was a translation device that would actually wire itself directly into the language centers of my brain so I could understand every language in the galaxy. It had seemed impossible, until now.

"Rager." His name suited him. His hands rested on his thighs—his powerful, big thighs—and I couldn't miss how large they were. Yes, everything about him was *big*. My eyes widened. "You're my mate?"

His golden eyes softened to something that made my nipples harden instantly. There was more than just lust there. I wasn't quite sure what, but my body reacted as if he'd just given me an hour-long massage. Was I turning into a puddle? Right now? "I mean, um. Wow. Nice to meet you."

I held out my right hand and he looked confused for a moment before enveloping it in his much larger one. He held my palm in his, the fingertips of his other hand stroked my arm, the inside of my wrist, and I bit my lip as heat engulfed me. Not just from him, but from the other four hands that still touched me, helping me remain upright.

So hot. God, I couldn't breathe.

Tearing my gaze from Rager's, I couldn't help but hope that everything on him was *big*. I licked my lips at the possibility. My mate? He was gorgeous.

He grinned then and I swear I felt my ovaries jump for joy. Wow. I couldn't believe this guy was my mate? The one I'd been matched to? I'd sat in the testing chair earlier and had this really hot dream. A sex dream where I was tied up and taken. Yes, taken. Rough and hard, gentle and wild. Things I'd never done, positions I only wished I'd tried before. And I'd felt so damn good. I'd actually come not once, not twice, but three times before Warden Egara had cruelly woken me. My pussy had been so needy and wet the back of my testing gown had been soaked.

The last few months in that stupid prison cell hadn't helped curb my need for a good, hard orgasm. I'd always enjoyed sex, or at least not been one of those women who was afraid to tell my lover what I wanted, or how I liked to be touched. The trouble, aside from there not there being any men available to sleep with in the all-women's prison, was that even on the outside, a lot of guys just didn't listen.

I'd been approached by several lesbians on the inside, and I'd considered it. But seriously? I loved men. I loved the way their shoulders hulked over me as we fucked, loved their smell, their strength. I loved the way I felt small and at my lover's mercy. Not that I'd ever talked about *that*, but I knew. I wanted a man, a dominant, take-charge lover with a big, hard cock and the patience to make me scream.

If this hot alien was my reward for breaking the law, I should have done it a couple of years ago instead of putting up with those lying assholes stealing my code and swatting me on the ass when I walked by. They hadn't all been bad, but man, a couple bad apples was all it took to ruin the place for everyone who worked there. Especially the women. Two years after the doors opened, I'd been the only woman left.

The information I leaked cost them their IPO, and landed me in jail for insider trading, but I'd been beyond caring. Sure, I could have served my two years and gone on. But then...this.

A mate. A fresh start with the Interstellar Brides Program.

The past was the past. Here I was on an alien world surrounded by hot men. I'd figured I'd get an average guy—alien—from some nice planet to take care of me the rest of my life. I knew from bride program ads and TV commercials that the testing would match me, using various personality and subconscious analysis, to a specific planet. From there, I'd be matched to the perfect mate. But I'd had doubts, the same ones I'd had ever since I became interested in sex. Maybe even before then when I longed to be tied up, to be told what to do by a commanding man, even when I hadn't understood that interest.

I mean, what guy from another planet would be able to handle my crazy sexual desires? Yeah, I was wired differently than other women. I'd known that since high school when I wasn't a shy, timid virgin—even when I had been a virgin. My sex drive was higher than other women. I came three times in a testing dream, which, per the Warden, was not normal. So what if I had hot buttons some men hadn't even wanted to try to push? So what if my inhibitions were low? Pretty much, I'd been called a slut, a freak, a whore. I was none of those things, but it hadn't mattered. No man had ever wanted me for more than a quick fling, a one-night stand, and it hadn't ever been that great. So I'd gotten off the damn planet and now here I was. On Viken.

With him.

"Rager," I repeated, tracing his full lips with my gaze as I imagined running my fingers through his hair. I couldn't tell exactly how tall he was, but I was pretty damn sure my five-six wouldn't even reach his chin.

Hot. So hot.

He nodded once, then angled his head toward the other two. "This is Evon."

The hard-ass blond nodded.

"And Liam." The black-haired man with stormy-blue eyes.

The first looked like a hard-ass Navy SEAL, the second like a pirate.

The two men still had their hands on me, were still eyeing me like they'd just captured their prey. It seemed odd these two were touching me when Rager was my mate.

"Tell us if you are hurt." Evon didn't ask a question, he demanded information and I complied instinctively, wanting to please him for some strange, completely unknown reason I didn't have time to analyze.

"I'm fine," I said. "I just want to get up off the flo—"

Before I could finish my sentence, Liam—the long,

raven-haired hottie—scooped me up into his arms and stood.

"Eep," I said, gripping onto his biceps with one hand and pressing against his chest with the other, worried he'd drop me. Good god, the man was made out of steel. Hot steel. I could feel the sinew of his muscles, corded and well-honed beneath my fingers. There was no way he was going to drop me. Hell, the secure way he held me, I wasn't sure if he was going to ever put me down. I licked my lips, wondering what all that expanse of torso would look like bare.

Before me stood the blond man. His hair was cropped short, close to his head, and his pale blue eyes were cold as ice, his focus absolute. On me.

"I'm Evon. Your other mate."

My mouth fell open.

"I would like to hear you speak my name as well."

"Evon. My other mate?" I asked. Was that a squeak in my voice? Thank god I wasn't ogling the guy who held me as if I weighed a feather—not—while my matched mate, Rager, stood by. I knew I found men attractive, but this was beneath even me. I was a one-man woman. I might like sex, but monogamy was my thing. I wasn't a cheater.

"You have three mates," Evon said, placing his palm on the side of my hip and offering a gentle squeeze. "And I would like to know how you say your name."

"The report says, 'Eye-zee-bee-la'?" Rager stood with a tablet of some sort in his hand, his brows drawn together in confusion. "I do not know this language."

"I'm Bella. My name is Isabella Maria Santiago Martinez, but my friends call me Bella."

"We are not your friends." Evon spoke again, lifting a

hand to stroke my cheek. "We are your mates. And you are Bella. Our Bella."

I turned my head to look up at Liam who was watching me with complete acceptance of Evon's words clearly written across his face. He had the gorgeous long black hair, like a Native American's, sleek and smooth, almost blue beneath the industrial lighting. His eyes, several shades deeper than Evon's, looked at me. No, he didn't look. He didn't stare. His gaze bore into me as if he could see more than just my face and the odd white dress I wore. I felt like he was peering into my very soul, stripping me bare without lifting a finger. Like he owned me.

Nearly panicked now, I shifted in his arms to find Rager walking toward us. He'd put the tablet down somewhere and all three men surrounded me once more. I searched his gaze for disagreement. Three big brutes like this would never share a woman where I came from. Frankly, I doubted they were capable of it. What if I preferred one over the other? What if I fell in love and the other two got jealous? What if they wanted to pass me around like property and they all had other mates, other women, hidden somewhere.

"Holy shit," I muttered and tried to wiggle out of Liam's grasp. I was in big trouble here. "Three? There was no mention of three. There must be some mistake. This will never work."

Liam shook his head, squeezed me impossibly tighter to him and his eyes darkened with something that made me shiver, and not with heat. That look shocked me and made me feel safe at the same time. It was a look that said he'd kill to keep me, and protect me. "No, there is no mistake. Now that you are here, we are not letting you go."

"But I was to be matched to the one man, the one alien,

who was...um, supposed to be perfect for me." I couldn't hold his gaze, but when I looked away, Evon's glacier-blue eyes were there, waiting to trap me.

His pale brow arched as he looked down at me. "You *have* been matched to the mates who are perfect for you."

Rager grunted agreement and walked toward a large sliding door. Liam, with me in his arms, followed. Evon fell into step beside us. I wiggled in protest, but Liam didn't even glance down at me, simply tightened his hold until I got the message.

No. I would not be walking yet.

I knew I should protest, but something inside me was unfurling from a long sleep, and that wicked, wicked woman wanted to know what it would be like to be with three of the hottest men she'd ever seen. Ever. She wanted to be between them, taking everything they could give her... even as she wondered just how much that was.

Liam continued to walk, but didn't need to see where he was going. The hall was straight and Rager was in front of us, leading the way...to somewhere. Liam's deep voice rumbled through my body and I settled in his arms, content. "You have three mates, Bella. Rager, Evon, me. We were tested and each of us matched to you. To us, *you* are the alien, and you are perfect."

He was adamant—not just spouting bullshit he thought I wanted to hear—and because of this, I loved to hear his words. They were sweet to my ears, like a Shakespeare sonnet, but slightly ridiculous.

"You don't even know me," I countered. "Trust me, I'm far from perfect."

Evon walked beside us down the wide hall. "We don't know you, just as you don't know us. This is true. But the testing makes things different. Even before I knew your name, I knew you would find all three of us attractive, that your pussy would be weeping in welcome even while meeting us for the very first time."

I should have been appalled by his bold words. If some guy at a bar approached me and was audacious and arrogant enough to tell me my pussy was wet at the mere sight of him, I would have kneed him in the nuts.

But Evon was right, my pussy was wet. I was attracted to all three of them. Instantly. Could they smell my arousal? Was there a wet spot on the back of my outfit, this simple white nightgown-type dress? I knew I wasn't wearing underwear. I could feel the smooth slide of the silky fabric over my bare bottom too well.

"Do not be upset by his bold words," Liam reassured. "While Evon wasn't particularly subtle, you must admit you liked his honesty. I will give you that honesty as well. While you find us appealing to your Earth-born senses, you have completely fascinated us. Can you not feel my hard cock against your hip?"

I gasped then, focusing on Liam's body. He held me to him closely, scooped up like a damsel in distress, and I could feel a hard pipe against my hip. I hadn't thought it was his cock. I hadn't thought at all, for I had been concentrating on their words. But now? Shit, it felt like a gun or something. Not a cock.

"Where are you taking me?" I asked.

"You have made her timid," Rager said, looking over his shoulder at me, then waving his hand beside a door, which slid open silently. He stepped inside and we followed, not that I had any choice, held as I was in Liam's arms.

I grinned at Rager's choice of words. I wasn't timid. I was, perhaps, too bold.

They brought me into a large room and I realized it was very similar to a high-dollar hotel suite with a living area, table, dark green sofas and chairs that looked like the fabric was pure spun silk, and a bed chamber...with a bed large enough for a football team.

Or me and these three hulking aliens.

"Oh god." Now? We were going to do this now? As in, get naked and go horizontal on that gigantic bed? Sure, technically, according to what they'd said, I was their wife now, and they were mine. So, it was all legal. Legit. Right?

Not that I'd needed a ring on my finger to get it on before, but this? With these three? The thought was exhilarating and terrifying all at the same time. I wanted them, which was insane in and of itself. But I was also nervous. It was reassuring somehow to know they were mine. That I *belonged* to them.

But did they really belong to me? How was one woman supposed to keep three hot aliens satisfied? I mean, seriously. They were like sex-on-a-stick and I was, well, just me.

"Are you guys sure about this? That you want me? Because Warden Egara told me that mates never cheat. But I don't know how three of you could be happy with just me."

"Let us show you." Liam's voice had gone deep, the heat of his body like a blowtorch everywhere we touched. At his words, Evon's gaze locked on mine and he took his time looking me over, his gaze lingering everywhere I wanted him to touch.

My pussy clenched and my nipples pebbled into hard,

hot points. My heart raced, but my head? Oh, whoa, the thoughts spinning in circles up there were one hot mess.

Did I want them? Yes. Yes, I did. Should I want them? No. Not three men at once.

Bad. Bad. Bad. Bad. I was so going to hell for this. Assuming they had a hell on this planet.

And all of that might have succeeded in changing my mind if I actually believed in hell. Which I didn't. So that just left...desire. Lust. Six months of gray walls, a prison uniform, and other women trying to convince me I wasn't into men anymore.

Wrong. So, so wrong.

They let me look around but once I'd caught my breath, Liam leaned down and kissed me on top of my head. Rager came up to me so he stood directly before me and stroked a finger down my cheek. Evon moved in beside him so I was surrounded by towering males.

"Don't worry, mate. We're going to take care of you now."

My eyes drifted closed as six hands roamed my body with a reverence to their touch I'd never felt before. I relaxed in Liam's hold, didn't protest when he walked to the bed and settled me on it so I was kneeling on the soft surface. When he let go, I opened my eyes, surprised that even now, Rager was nearly as tall as I. The other two were half a head shorter, but still huge, at least six-six.

Did they know how to grow 'em on Viken or what?

"You're all mine? All three of you? And you want this? You actually want to share me?" I had to know for sure before I did this. "You're sure there's not some mistake?"

Evon walked forward to stand directly before me, his eyes, cold before, were now pure, blue fire. "Take off your dress, mate. We want to see what's ours."

Yeah, okay. No mistake, then.

That voice. God. I held his gaze as I lifted my hands to the back of my neck and released the clasp I'd felt pressing into my skin there.

The soft fabric slid down my body in a slow glide, like frosting melting in the hot sun, revealing what lay beneath.

"You're mine." Evon's declaration was followed by the searing heat of his hand on my hip. "Lift your arms above your head and hold them there, mate."

Again, I did as he asked—even after only knowing him a few minutes—my full breasts jutting forward on display. I didn't have a model's body, I was more couch potato than marathon runner, especially after six months in jail, but the way his eyes darkened with lust, I felt like a goddess, a powerful, desirable ruler of men.

These men.

"Is she not perfect?" he asked the others.

Liam and Rager both nodded agreement as Evon motioned them forward.

"Kiss her, Rager. Everywhere, just like you want to. Fill that hot mouth of hers with your cock. Liam, her ass is yours. Make sure she's ready."

"Um—" I said, not getting anything else out. Kiss her everywhere? My ass belonged to Liam? "Uh..."

"Fuck, Evon. I knew you were going to start giving orders," Liam complained, but he was grinning as he did so, as he turned me to the side so he could grab my wrists, lower them and hold them behind my back.

Restrained, panting, I knew that if I were a good girl I'd tell them to stop. Ask more questions. Take my time and get to know them before we had what amounted to an all-out orgy. No, an orgy meant everyone would have sex with everyone else. The way Evon was talking, *they* were all going to have sex with *me*.

But as Evon's hands cupped my bare breasts, Liam's commanding grip on my wrists reminded me that I was theirs now, theirs to conquer, theirs to fuck, and that knowledge broke me open as raw need flooded every cell of my body. I moaned. God, I couldn't hold it in. Was it this simple? Were they going to give me exactly what I needed, even when I wasn't exactly sure what that was anymore?

Liam climbed up on the bed behind me, tugging my hair with his free hand to expose my neck to his kiss. He kicked my legs wide and I fell back against him, completely under his control as Rager leaned forward and licked my pussy, lingering on the hard nub of my clit.

All thoughts of living by Earth's standards fled. To hell with that.

It seemed I was being claimed and there wasn't a damn thing I wanted to do about it.

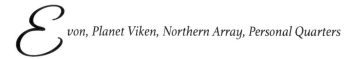

3

Evon, Planet Viken, Northern Array, Personal Quarters

OUR MATE WAS STUNNING. AND RESPONSIVE. RAGER HAD HIS head between her thighs and she was panting, her nipples tightening beneath my palms.

Gods, it was unbelievable. A female, sent from across the universe, and she was absolutely perfect for us. I'd doubted the matching, the testing, but no longer. I knew nothing of the planet Earth, whether she was of normal size, but to me, she was small. At least a foot shorter than any of us, it would be easy to overwhelm her. Harm her even. Her body was lush and curvy and I could discern supple muscles beneath her soft skin. She'd be equally soft everywhere, I was sure.

And the marks, the designs that were colorful and covered her arm, along one hip, I couldn't help but touch the delicate petals of a flower, the curved edge of a flying creature's wing. Rager pulled back and she whimpered, wiping his mouth with the back of his hand as he watched me. Bella sucked in a breath as I drew the tip of my finger over the patterns, ever so gently. Swirls of reds and blues, black and green. Some kind of Earth animal with wings, vines and flowers. A name? I pressed harder, to see if the color would bleed, but no.

"A tattoo," she said, her voice barely above a whisper. "It's ink, beneath my skin."

Liam and Rager looked, too. Intrigued.

"We do not have this...tattoo. I know of other planets who mark their bodies, but not with color or patterns such as these." I looked from the mark on her hip to her dark eyes. "What animal is this?"

She bit her lip and I knew then she enjoyed the barest of touches as I circled my finger. Even the littlest things were pleasing for her, and she hadn't even been affected by the seed power yet. The way her hips were shifting, Rager had done an excellent job of making her aroused, needy even. His mouth still glistened with her juices and I saw the way her thighs were slick.

"A butterfly."

Rager repeated the word as he leaned down, kissed the image on her skin. When she sucked in a breath this time, I watched as her breasts rose. I'd held them in my palms, heavy and full, but I'd become easily mesmerized by a simple tattoo.

"You have distracted me, mate."

She arched a brow, as if confused to how she'd done such a thing.

"I like control," I added.

Liam smiled at that, as if the three-word sentence was too modest to describe how I liked to fuck. It wasn't just me.

Everyone from Sector 2 demanded submission from their mates. It was in my blood. Because of the testing, it proved that Bella needed to submit.

"Do you like having your hands pinned by Liam?"

I saw her arms jerk as she tested his grip on her wrists, watched her pupils dilate knowing she wasn't getting free. We'd release her, of course, if she panicked, but that wasn't what I saw in her gaze. No, it was the complete opposite.

"I see you do. We will take you, push you, make you come. With three mates, there are many needs you must meet. Will *want* to meet."

"How can you be so sure?"

"Because we are your mates," Liam said, kissing her neck. He was the lucky bastard who had her in his arms, could feel the long line of her back, her bare skin.

"You are matched to us. Your needs match ours. Like a puzzle, our pieces connect. I like control, you like to be dominated."

I said it as fact. Her breathing was ragged and I could no longer ignore the way her teardrop-shaped breasts were thrust toward me. Her nipples had gone from lush brown tips to tight buds, the areolas dusky, wide circles on her full globes. Putting a knee on the bed, I bent down to take one in my mouth. The hard point pressed against my tongue and the roof of my mouth. Her skin was warm, her taste sweet, making my mouth water. She jerked, then stilled, knowing she could do nothing but take whatever we did to her.

Rager moved beside me, took her other nipple in his mouth. The two of us sucked and laved as Liam spoke to her.

"You see, having three mates, three lovers, is better than

one. While we will take our pleasure from your body, we will give you exactly what you need."

"Oh god," she breathed, and I felt a shudder run through her.

"Evon may demand your submission, but you will give it freely. See? I no longer hold your wrists, yet you keep them behind your back."

I hadn't known he'd released his hold, but my cock pulsed and throbbed, knowing she continued to be bound by our words.

"You want our mouths on your breasts, a hand on your pussy," Liam continued.

She cried out then, and I knew Liam's hand was touching her. He'd reached between her legs from behind. Glancing down, I saw the top of his fingers slide over her clit. Her pussy was bare and I couldn't miss the pink flesh, the little nub swell and come out from behind its hood by his touch.

I lifted my gaze, glanced over her shoulder at Liam. We didn't have to speak to know it was my turn to take over. I put my hand over Liam's on her pussy. His slid back and I covered her now, her flesh hot. Wet.

"Grasp your elbows," I said. Her dark eyes met mine, but they were blurry with need. Her shoulders moved, saw her elbows bend behind her back as she crossed her arms. The motion thrust her breasts out more, a feast for Rager. "Good girl. Now Liam can play with your ass. It's his favorite thing."

Her eyes widened and her mouth fell open as Liam cupped her ass with one hand, parted her cheeks and touched her. His fingers had to be slick with her juices— mine were drenched—as he began to play with her ass.

"Ever been fucked here?" Liam asked, leaning down and nipping the juncture of her neck and shoulder.

She shook her head and I was surprised. Liam's eyes lit up as if he were given the best present in the world.

"I've...I've played," she admitted. "Toys, but that's it."

"Then I will be your first," he promised.

I watched as her eyes filled with wariness, and while Liam couldn't see, he sensed it. "Not now. Soon. First, we play. We will learn every inch of your body and make you come. Only when you are begging will we fuck your pussy. And later, when your ass has been properly prepared, I'll fuck you there, too."

"You're all still dressed," she said, eyeing me and glancing down at Rager. He continued to lick and suck at her nipples, alternating between them, as if he wasn't sure which one needed the most attention. He was the patient one, content to savor our mate's body for hours. No doubt he would get her to come from his attentions alone if given long enough.

He lifted his head then, though, grinning. "You want to see us?"

She nodded.

Rager and I moved to stand before her, Liam crawling off the bed so we were side by side. Then we stripped off our uniforms. They were identical except for color. Mine black, Liam's brown and Rager's steel gray, signifying our birth Sector. I watched her eyes as she took us in, not knowing where to look. While we were of similar height, nothing else about us was the same. I was light, Liam dark. Rager was broader, heavier.

Once our clothes were strewn at our feet, I gripped my cock at the base, staved off my need for her. I could come just by looking at her before us, up on her knees, her legs parted so her pussy was visible. Her nipples wet and hard from Rager's mouth, her hands behind her back.

"She's perfect," Rager murmured. I saw out of the corner of my eye that he, too, was stroking his cock.

She licked her lips as she stared at my cock, then Rager's, then Liam's.

"Like what you see?" Liam asked.

Transfixed, she nodded.

I felt a bead of pre-cum seep from my tip and I rubbed it with my thumb. "You've been mated to three warriors, yet we're also Viken." I let go of my cock so it bounced against my belly, stepped closer, swiped my wet thumb over her nipple, painting it with my pre-cum. I watched, waited.

She'd lowered her head to see what I was doing. It was a simple gesture, perhaps odd for her. When she lifted her head, her eyes were wide, her mouth open. They went from a focused dark brown to blurry. Her nipples went instantly soft and she dropped down onto her heels.

"Oh my god," she murmured, a shiver running through her.

Rager did the same thing, swiped his finger over her other breast, coated it with a drop of his own pre-cum. Her arms fell to her sides and her eyes closed.

"What...what is that?" she asked. "What's happening to me?"

Liam was the last to coat her with his pre-cum, walking up to her and brushing his thumb over her bottom lip. Her pink tongue darted out, tasted it.

All at once, her eyes flared open, her body jerked and stiffened, then she screamed.

"Fuck," I breathed, watching as she came. Hard. We

weren't even touching her. She shifted her hips, as if trying to find a cock to ride. Her breasts bounced and swayed, her skin flushed from her cheeks all the way down her neck. Her head fell back, her long hair swaying against her back.

I glanced at Rager, who now held his cock once again, squeezing it hard at the base to stave off his own orgasm. She collapsed back onto the bed, her head on the pillow as she tried to catch her breath and stared up at us. Her eyes were glazed with pleasure, softer than they'd been before. Accepting. And I wanted to keep her right there, on the edge, needy, mindless. It would be easy to do now.

Rager didn't wait. He stalked up the bed, grabbed hold of her ankles and parted her wide. I could see her pussy, swollen and wet, just before Rager lowered his head and devoured her. She cried out again, her back arching, her head thrown back. He'd had a quick taste before, but he was ready for a full meal now.

Liam went around the bed to the far side, came to sit beside her. I went to her near side, knelt on the floor so I was leaning and whispering in her ear. I breathed in her scent, almost floral. It was mixed with a tang of sweat and her arousal. It was the most powerful aphrodisiac. My cock pressed against the side of the bed, aching.

"What just happened? The way you came, just like that? Seed power. Powerful, isn't it? It's strong, the need for your mates now coursing through your veins. You came, just from the barest touch of our seed, which is quite rare. Since you can come from that alone, imagine, mate, what it will feel like now, when we get our hands on you, our cocks into you, when we fill you up. What it will ultimately be like when we officially claim you, all three of us fucking you at the same time."

Moaning as Rager worked her with his mouth, her hips bucked. Rager lifted his head just long enough to say three words.

"Hold her open."

Immediately, Liam and I complied, each of us lifting a hand to one knee and pulling her thighs up toward her chest, her legs spread, her wet, pink pussy tilted up to Rager for easy access. Liam returned his attention to her nipple and she arched her back, pushing up toward his mouth. She lowered her hands to his head and tangled her fingers in his long, black hair, holding him to her, but I wouldn't allow that. She was not in control here. I was.

She would take what we gave her and make no demands. We would make her scream, give her pleasure she'd never known. We would conquer her body...on our terms.

I grabbed her wrists with my free hand and raised them above her head, satisfied as I watched her gaze flood with heat and she moaned, twisting in our hold, but Liam and I held firm as her breathing increased and she closed her eyes in surrender. She couldn't move. Couldn't do anything but submit to Rager's wicked tongue.

With a grin, Rager dipped his head once more and I watched, transfixed as he slowly slid his tongue into her wet pussy, fucking her with his mouth as he worked her clit with his fingers.

"More seed power, Rager. Rub your pre-cum all over her clit."

"Oh god." Bella turned her head toward me and opened her eyes.

"Kiss me," she whispered. "Please."

Thrilled that she'd asked, I lowered my lips to hers, my

arms still wide, holding her in place as Rager worked her with his mouth. His earlier groan of pleasure was now a growl as his control threatened to slip. I was pushing him, pushing us all, and I relished the razor's edge, the thin line of control, taking us all to the brink. My lips hovering above hers, I gave an order. "You'll come all over Rager's face, then we'll fuck you."

Perhaps it was my words, or Rager's attentions, but she came again as I took her mouth, swallowed her cries of pleasure. She tasted like softness and light, like flowers and candy.

Mine.

The thought was primal, but I didn't resist it as I pushed into her, claiming the sweet recesses of her mouth as my own. She was all mine, with Rager and Liam. This was my family now. Mine to command, to control, to pleasure.

She whimpered and opened to me as she came. It wasn't a hard come, but a soft one, her body going lax, goose bumps rising on her flesh as she whimpered, rode the wave of pleasure.

Rager lifted his head, but kept hold of her ankles and tugged. I released my grip, letting her move where Rager wished. She slid easily down the bed so her ass was on the edge, her lower legs over Rager's shoulders. He stood and her legs slid down until he held her ankles at his shoulders. Her pussy was up off the mattress, but aligned perfectly with his cock. "I'm first."

I looked down into her eyes and she stared up at me in complete surrender. Whatever I said, whatever I wanted, would be mine.

The knowledge made me so hard I winced in pain as my cock jumped. Rager was more beast than the rest of us, but his need to taste her had been appeased. He would wait. It was Liam who neared the breaking point now, but his release would be all the sweeter for being forced to hold off. Just as I would care for my mate, I needed to be sure my brothers-in-arms' needs were met. I was the strongest of will, the darkest of mind. I would wait, even if my cock didn't agree.

"Fuck her, Rager. Fuck her and fill her with your seed."

Her ankles were raised up to his shoulders, his weeping cock perfectly aligned.

He looked to me and I nodded. "Just a moment, Rager. Wait for me to spread her pussy open, then fuck her slowly. I want to watch her take you deep, see her face as you fill her."

Rager groaned as he eyed Liam suckling our mate's beautiful breasts.

I lowered my hand to her swollen pussy lips and clenched my jaw in sweet agony as the wet heat of her coated my fingers. Gods, she was perfect. Looking down into her eyes, I clenched one hand in her long, black hair and angled her face up to look at me. "Look at me as he fucks you, mate. Look into my eyes. Don't look away."

She blinked and I knew she heard me because her gaze locked onto mine, nearly mindless but full of trust and want. I wanted more, I realized, in that moment, that I needed to see more. Tenderness? Affection? Love? Emotions we had not earned from our little mate. It was too soon. But we would. I was determined. She would love us. She must. We needed her far more than she needed us. She was the only light in our dark existence. Ours.

"You are beautiful, Bella." As I spoke, I used the fingers of my other hand to spread open her pussy lips and hold them wide, exposing her empty core, spreading her for Rager's cock. She gasped and arched off the bed, angling herself so he would fill her, but I was having none of that. She was not in control here, and she would soon understand. "Liam, lock her down."

Liam's arm slid over her waist, holding her hips and chest down on the bed. She moaned, her pussy clenching so hard I could feel it in my fingertips as I held her open wide. I looked at her, waiting a moment to ensure she was with us, that she wanted this. Yes, she wanted everything we were giving her. Taking. "Now, Rager. Slowly."

He slid into her body one slow inch at a time. She tried to buck and take more of him, but I pushed down with the thick part of my palm over her clit and tightened my fist in her hair.

"Oh god, oh god, oh god!" She panted the words, but she held my gaze as I'd ordered. Liam's sucking intensified on her breast and he moved his head up and down like a machine, pulling and tugging her nipple with his mouth as Rager pushed forward until he was buried to the balls.

"Don't move, Rager. Don't fuck her. I want her to come like this." I slid my hand up until my fingertips rested over her clit and pinched, pulled, tugged. Her quivering turned to trembles, then muscles spasms as she lost control.

"Fuck, Evon. I can't hold back." Rager's growling voice made me grin as Bella's hot pussy fisted his cock, milked him of his seed. He tensed, every line of his body hard as he came. Pumped into her. Filled her up.

I watched, knowing the seed power in Rager's cum would hit her hard. I would have only seconds, I knew, if I wanted to be balls deep when her next orgasm raced through her body.

"My turn," I growled.

Rager slid from her body, his cock glistening with her wetness and we traded places. But this wasn't enough for me. I needed more.

I lifted her hips from the bed and thrust hard and deep as the seed power of Rager's release flooded her bloodstream. She exploded again, her legs wrapping around my hips, pulling me deeper as her pussy clenched and spasmed around me. Gods, she felt incredible. Hot, wet and tight, her walls rippled around me. And I wasn't even moving. Drowning in pleasure, I noticed her hand was once again buried in Rager's hair.

Rager knelt at her side where I'd been, stroking her body with a gentle slide of his fingertips over her flesh. I watched, imagined the sensation to distract myself and hold on. I wasn't ready to come yet. I wanted to fuck her. I *needed* to conquer her, break down her barriers, *break* her until she was a thoughtless, mindless puddle of sensation and need. No thoughts. No doubts. Just us. Just pleasure.

"Lift her to my chest," I ordered, and Liam and Rager moved to comply. They lifted her into my arms so we were chest to chest, her legs wrapped around my hips as I held her to me, impaled on my cock. I nodded to Liam. "Get her ready for you, Liam."

His eyes lit with a nearly fanatical gleam as he walked to a concealed drawer in the suite and pulled a small box from the wall. Still panting, Bella turned to watch him, distracted. She'd already come twice.

I lowered my hands to her rounded ass and lifted her, then slammed her down on my cock. She cried out, her attention returning to me as I thrust up into her over and over in small strokes designed to drive her wild. She clung to me, melting into my arms and something inside me relaxed, nearly content. It was a feeling that put me on edge, one I hadn't felt in years...if ever. Not like this. I hadn't felt this warmth in my heart since before the wars, before I'd lost faith.

Bella was going to break me. Make me weak, even as I held her, safe and secure in my arms.

Annoyed with my lack of focus, I pushed those thoughts aside and walked to the side of the bed. Keeping her chest pressed to mine, I sat down on the edge then leaned back until I was lying flat with Bella draped over me like a blanket. My legs remained bent over the edge, feet on the floor as my curvy mate straddled me. She was on top of me now, her knees pressed to the soft mattress on either side of my hips, and she tried to move, to rub her sensitive little clit against my hard body. But I held her in place, her round bottom up in the air, my hands locked onto her hips as I tugged on the firm globes, pulled her wide, forcing apart her sweet little ass.

"Fill her up, Liam. Get her ready for your cock."

4

EVON WAS UNDER ME, FILLING ME, HIS HANDS ON MY BOTTOM as I lay sprawled across his chest. I buried my face against his hard flesh, taking in his masculine scent. Our bodies were damp with sweat, the pungent scent of sex filled the air. So did the wet sound of it as I rode his cock.

My legs were open as I straddled him, fucked him. He was so strong, so damn bossy. Everything he said, the others did. Hell, I did. He used that tone of voice and I melted. Even thinking about it made my pussy pulse and I sank down just a little more, pulling him deeper. He was so big, the same with Rager, although one was longer, the other thicker. We both groaned and I bit his salty skin, not hard, just enough to let him know he was mine. I didn't know why I did it, and I didn't care. I wanted to mark him, just as they were marking me with their seed.

And that seed power thing? I had no idea what it was, but I wanted more. It felt like I'd gotten a shot of morphine, but better. I wasn't in a drug-induced haze. No, it was sex-induced. I'd never felt so instantly aroused. Not just aroused. It had actually made me come. I didn't understand it and now wasn't the time to figure it out. Not with Evon's cock deep inside me and with what Liam planned to do.

"Harder, mate."

I knew more was coming, knew soon I'd be overwhelmed once again, but Evon was my anchor in this storm and I clung to him. Needed him already. I'd never felt so out of control, or so safe. My confusion was real, and as I felt Liam move into place behind me, Evon's strong hands on my ass, pulling me open for my other mate, I began to panic.

In an instant, Evon softened his hold, soothing me with long, slow strokes of his palms up and down my back. "You are ours, mate. And we will never take you without permission. We will never do something you do not wish, do not like. One word, Bella. One word and everything stops."

I'd heard of safe words on Earth, but this felt so different. So...dangerous. How far would they push me? Just how far would I let them go? I didn't know. And I was more afraid of myself at the moment than my new mates. I'd never had anyone—let alone three anyones—give me as much as I could handle, or more. "What word?"

"No. Don't. Stop. They all work," Evon said. "If you utter any of them, everything stops."

I nodded and shifted my hips forward and back, trying to ride him once more. Tingling heat was spreading through my pussy and I recognized it now, the fire of their seed power. It was like a drug and I knew Evon's pre-cum was coating my pussy walls, just as Rager's seed had, sinking into my system, making me hot and needy. God, if they could bottle this stuff on Earth, they'd be millionaires overnight. "I want you to fill me up. Come inside me."

Evon's hands returned to my bottom and he lifted his hips, ramming up into my weeping pussy. Hard.

I barely recognized the whimper that came out of my throat, but I was done trying to figure this thing out. I had three mates now. And I hoped this wouldn't be the last time I was between them.

Evon pulled on the soft flesh of my bottom. My pussy and ass both felt open and exposed as Liam's fingers came to rest on my virgin hole. "I'm going to fill that sweet ass with a toy, Bella. Get you ready for me."

Even as he spoke, his fingers circled, coated me in lube, then pressed. I groaned, but he easily slipped inside.

"Oh god," I moaned. I had Evon in my pussy and Liam's finger in my ass. I'd never felt so filled, but I knew this was just the start. Liam's finger moved inside me, spreading something slippery around and inside my tight hole. It was warming and very slick. Some kind of space lube.

"Squeeze us, mate," Evon demanded as Liam pulled one finger back, then two inside.

Holy. Shit.

I dropped my head forward once more, pulling Evon's flesh into my mouth. I sucked on his skin hard, wanting to leave a visible mark on him as they were leaving their mark on my soul. I would never be the same, not after this. They would own me. I sucked and bit, hard, lightning and power coursing through my body as Evon's hand fisted in my hair and he moaned beneath me, bucking harder.

I released him and inspected my work, a deep, abiding

satisfaction coursing through me when I saw the bright strawberry on his skin. Mine. That mark meant he was mine.

I wanted to mark all of them. They were *mine.* I wanted everyone to know it and I wasn't going to share. Was it the seed power that made me all at once fiercely possessive?

That was my last coherent thought because Liam moved, filling me with his fingers, pulling out. Spreading me open, making my pussy that much tighter. Fuller.

Evon and Liam fucked me together, Liam timing his movements to be opposite the hard thrusts of Evon's cock in my pussy, mimicking what I knew they would do when he ultimately claimed my ass.

"Rager, take over for Liam," Evon commanded. "Fill her with a training plug and spank her if she disobeys."

"What?" I nipped him again, harder. But he only groaned and pushed my mouth down into his chest for more. God, he was so fucking hot. He wanted more. He wanted my mark on his skin. My brand. I bounced on his cock and spread my legs as wide as they would go, until my hips threatened to cramp. Even that pain made me burn. Hotter.

God, I was so messed up right now. But I didn't care. I couldn't stop. I wanted more. Maybe it was the seed power. Maybe it was freedom after long months in jail. Maybe it was just them. I didn't know. Didn't care. I needed.

Lifting my head, I nibbled on Evon's jaw. His neck. He tasted like sin, hot musky male. "I need more. Please. More."

"Liam, our mate is talking too much. Fuck her mouth."

Forehead pressed to Evon's heat, I tried to ignore the sound of shuffling feet, of movement, the dip of the bed as Liam crawled onto the mattress beside me. I knew when I opened my eyes and lifted my head that his cock would be close. And that Evon expected me to swallow Liam down even as the other two fucked me down below.

I could tell him no. Say the words. *No. Don't. Stop.* And they would. But there was Liam's thick cock bobbing before me, the large crown a ruddy red, pre-cum seeping from the narrow slit and all at once my mouth watered, eager to taste him.

"Now, mate." Evon's hand tightened in my hair and he lifted my head until my mouth was level with Liam's waiting cock. He knelt beside us on the bed, his knees at Evon's shoulders. "Open that sweet mouth and suck him down."

His grip was so tight it stung, my eyes automatically watering at the slight pain, but that sting travelled straight to my clit and I opened my mouth with a soft cry, eager for the taste of my other mate, to lick up that pre-cum.

Bracing myself with my hands on Evon's shoulders, I leaned to the side and swallowed him down until he hit the back of my throat. He was huge, but I closed my lips around him and sucked, hard. I moaned.

Liam's shout was my reward and I sucked harder, holding my breath, stroking him with my tongue for as long as I could. When the need for oxygen forced me to release him, I slid back quickly, drew in a lungful of air and took him again.

Evon used the hand in my hair to help guide me, thrusting me forward and pulling me back as I worked Liam's cock. I refused to let him go, to allow him even a moment's reprieve from the pressure, the tight suction of my mouth.

Behind me, Rager worked a plug of some type into my ass, each round section pushing past my tight muscle with a distinct pop that made my pussy clench around Evon's cock like a fist. I had no idea how big it was; I couldn't see anything but Liam's glorious cock.

Three men? Fuck, yeah. If I'd known it was going to be like this, I wouldn't have waited. I'd have volunteered for the Brides Program sooner. These three, they'd been waiting for me, just as I had them. We just hadn't known it.

"Make him come, mate," Evon growled. "Make him come and swallow him down."

Evon thrust in earnest now, bucking beneath me on the edge of his own tight control. The knowledge thrilled me and I pushed him further, lifting one hand to stroke Liam's balls, forcing Evon to hold my head, direct me with the strength of his grip in my hair.

"Slow down, mate," Evon ordered, but I refused to listen. I had Liam on the edge, and I was going to push him over, take control, force him to give me what I wanted. I squeezed my inner muscles around Evon's cock, tight. Hard. In a rhythm I knew would drive him over the edge.

"Spank her, Rager. She's not listening."

Rager's hand landed on my bare bottom with a sharp crack of sound, the sting hitting half a second later.

Instead of discouraging me, my body jerked and shook. Holy shit. The sting turned to heat, like lava in my blood and lightning to my clit.

I bucked on Evon's cock and locked my lips around Liam's, squeezing his balls, twisting slightly, pulling on them as he shoved his hard length down my throat. I was on the brink of coming. One cock in my mouth, one in my pussy, a toy in my ass. A spanking.

"Again. Don't stop until she behaves."

Behaves? If being a bad girl felt like this, I had no intention of behaving.

Rager's palm swatted me again and again, the heat spreading, blooming. If Evon thought this was going to make me stop, he was sorely mistaken.

The heat built inside me, spreading until I felt like a bomb about to explode.

Liam lost control first, his hands in my hair, holding me, as his cum exploded down my throat, coating me with his seed. I swallowed him down as the tingling started. As the seed power overwhelmed.

Shoving on his hip so I could breathe, I cried out as Rager spanked me again and again. I rode Evon's cock as the rush of Liam's seed power moved through me in a wave better than any drug. It made me shake, made me crazed. But I couldn't come. Couldn't let go. I was waiting for something. I *needed* something else.

Evon released my hair, both hands returning to my hips as he lifted his body off the bed, rocketing into my swollen pussy, hard and fast. "Come now, Bella. Come all over my cock."

That was it. Command. My body responded as if he'd pressed a button and I screamed, Rager's hand landing with one final swat as Evon filled me with his seed. My body jerked and twisted, out of my control as I writhed on top of my mate, milking his cock, taking everything. It was beyond bliss. Colors danced and swirled behind my closed eyelids. I tasted Liam's cum on my tongue, felt it spurt hotly from Evon deep inside me. Shit. It was insane, this feeling. My skin was sensitive, my nipples aching points, my clit hard and swollen. Inside my pussy, my G-spot and every other spot pulsed. I couldn't breathe and I swear I was going to black out if it felt any better.

Only when Liam wiped the corner of my mouth with his thumb was I able to catch my breath. The need still simmered, but I was sated. For now.

Evon held me in place on top of him and I heard the other two shuffling around. The toy was carefully removed from my ass. I came again, only slightly when the little bumps of the toy popped out. I whimpered against Evon, too worn out to do anything more. The sounds of washing and soft male voices as Liam and Rager cleaned up drifted to me. They soon joined us on the bed.

Ignoring everything, I waited for my heart to slow and my body to cool. It took too long, aftershocks zinging my pussy and clit with smaller orgasms as the seed power flooded my bloodstream. I didn't have the strength to move, but with Evon's cock still buried deep, my pussy didn't need much to spasm, over and over as I lay exhausted atop my mate's broad chest.

I lost track of time as my body recovered. The steady beat of Evon's heart a soothing balm to my wrecked body.

How was I going to continue this? Three mates. How often were we going to get naked like this? It was too much, too intense. I wouldn't survive.

"I don't think I can do this." A tear slipped from my eye, and Evon's hands, one stroking my hair, one moving in a tender caress up and down my back, stilled.

"Are you unwell? Did we hurt you?" His voice was not commanding now, but filled with a vulnerability even I could recognize.

"No. It's just...too much. Too intense."

He sighed and his hands resumed the calming motion,

soothing me, making me feel loved. Which I knew was impossible, since I'd only met these aliens, my mates, an hour ago. But the illusion was nice and warm and safe, and so I let myself roll in the feeling. In him.

In them.

The mattress dipped again, and Evon pulled his cock from me with a sigh, shifting us up toward the top of the bed. There, on either side of him, were my other two mates.

Three. And as I looked from one to the next, they all had the same expression in their eyes. Devotion. Possession. Obsession.

Yeah, I was in a helluva lot of trouble here.

"The seed power from just one Viken can be overpowering during a mating, Bella. You have three."

I cleared my throat and looked at Rager with his beautiful bronze hair and warm eyes. "You mean I'm overdosing on orgasms? What, exactly, does this seed power do? Other than make me so horny I can't think straight."

Silent and steady, Evon continued to stroke my back, soothing me with his gentle touch. On my other side, Liam chuckled but answered the question.

"Viken men have a bonding chemical in our seed that helps us pleasure our women, bond them to us more quickly and completely."

So, they had a cheat? One little drop of that stuff and their women started having orgasms like they were hiccups. Unstoppable. Powerful.

Addictive.

"That's cheating, you know."

Evon's hands stilled on my back and his deep voice rumbled through me. "We are ruthless, mate. When it comes to you, we will do whatever we must to keep you safe and happy by our sides."

Holy shit. I should have been freaked out, at least a little. A few hours ago, I'd been an independent, single woman. Before landing in jail, I'd been powerful in my own right, a programmer and hacker. I wasn't stupid, and I wasn't used to depending on a man for...well, anything. Not even my pleasure. I'd found my vibrator to be a more consistent and trustworthy form of release than any man.

But now? Here I was, wrung out on orgasms, surrounded by not one, but three of the biggest, hottest alien men I could ever imagine. And they all looked at me like I was the sun and stars, their whole world.

It was surreal. Too much to process. I closed my eyes and allowed the exhaustion of transport, and our mating, to drag me under. Surrounded by my mates, I felt safe.

5

"WHY DID YOU VOLUNTEER TO BE A BRIDE?" I ASKED. AFTER the sweaty bout of fucking—gods, it had been incredible—we'd all fallen asleep. If Bella hadn't spoken at the end, I would have thought her falling unconscious from pleasure.

She shook her head, her sleek hair falling over her shoulder. I tucked it back behind her ear as she spoke, my longing to touch her so deep I could not stop, not for a moment. "I didn't. Well, I did, but not exactly." Her dark eyes met mine. "I...um, thought you guys knew about me."

Her eyes closed as she pressed her cheek into my hand and contentment flooded me for the first time in long years. Perhaps ever. I couldn't help the grin that split my face. I felt good. Not just because Bella's mouth was pure heaven or that she'd sucked the cum from my balls, but because she was here. With us. Between us.

She was mine now, my mate, my purpose for breathing and fighting. Honor had kept me on my chosen path these long years, but this was something different and much more powerful. She was mine to cherish and protect. This was personal, and that changed everything.

Having blood relatives, alive and on the same planet, didn't make them family. I'd once belonged, a long-awaited son, but I'd turned my back on my past when my family disowned me, when they refused to see reason, refused to believe a united planet was crucial to our future survival in the Coalition. My father was still a leader of the Viken Sector Separatists movement. He spoke at VSS rallies and stirred up trouble. My entire family believed the Viken should separate from the Interstellar Coalition and return to autonomous rule of our own planet.

But they hadn't seen what I had. They'd never faced down a Hive Scout or encountered a friend who'd once been whole and was now nothing more than a walking cyborg mind, connected to their core control, unable to think or walk or act alone. There was nothing left of the man inside that machine shell.

The Hive destroyed everything it touched, devoured entire civilizations. My father refused to believe the threat was as severe as the Coalition claimed. He'd lost a daughter to the Interstellar The Colony when she'd volunteered to escape his fanatical views, matched to Atlan, a planet far from Viken. And he'd lost me when I'd been caught vandalizing a government building. I'd set the damn thing on fire late at night, convinced by my father that rooting out the Coalition supporters was the only way to win our freedom.

I'd been a fool, just a teenager on the edge of adulthood, desperate to do anything to please my father.

Being young, and foolish, I'd agreed and been caught. Processed by our justice system, I'd been given two choices, years of confinement or service in the Coalition Fleet. I'd grown up out there, in space, facing monsters my father had spent my entire youth insisting weren't real.

They were very real. And now I was alone, except for Rager and Evon. We'd been friends for years. So close that we'd agreed to share a mate per the kings' and queen's wishes. With Bella ours now, we were a new family. My family. And I would allow nothing to separate us.

Our seed power ensured our new mate would want to remain close—and eager for us—so we would have time to woo her, to win her heart even as we conquered her body. Inside me, a small painful ticking tormented me without end. And I knew I would find no relief from this uncertainty until she accepted us officially and claimed us. Until then, she had thirty days to change her mind, to walk away from us. To leave us behind and choose another mate.

My stomach dropped at the idea and I reached out to stroke the curve of her hip. We were on our sides, facing one another, Rager spooned against her back. Evon had gone to the food unit for sustenance. The way her cheeks were flushing again, the way her eyes had that eager, needy look in them, we'd be wise to take sustenance now, to feed her and care for her before her body demanded more attention from one of us, or all of us, in turn.

While we had jobs to do, her arrival afforded us immediate

leave. We had days, perhaps even a week to claim her before we would be forced to return to our scheduled shifts. I didn't want to be parted from her, not even for a moment. Not yet. Too soon our duties as guardians of the Interstellar Quantum Communications Array would impede on this time we had together. I would be required to leave her side, to trust her care to another. I couldn't fathom the idea, not yet.

"So, you were not a volunteer for the Brides Program? How did you end up here?" Rager's hand slid down her arm and I watched as goose bumps rose on her skin. She appeared to be content lying between us, allowing us to explore her softness, her curves. She was not modest. I cupped her breast with my hand and she sighed, stretching with a grin on her face.

"I feel like a sleepy kitten." When she snuggled back into Rager's hold, his arm tightened around her waist and she rested her head on his biceps, looking up at me. "I don't think I can move."

I played with her hair, twirling the long black strands around my fingers, then splaying them over her bare breast. The effect was beautiful. Hypnotic. I could stare at her beauty for hours and never tire of looking. "What is a kitten?" I asked.

"A baby cat. They're cute and fuzzy and have extremely sharp claws." The last she said with a grin and I chuckled.

"And do you have sharp claws, mate?"

She arched a brow. "I used to. Now..." Her gaze wandered to the side and she raised a hand to my chest, petting me in turn. Her touch seared me to the depths of my soul like a brand and I knew I'd never get enough of her. "Now, here? I don't know."

Rager nuzzled the back of her neck. "So you did not

volunteer to be a bride. Tell us how you got here. We must know everything about you."

My thumb found its way to her plump bottom lip and I traced the soft curve. "Everything."

She nipped the tip of my thumb, which did nothing but make my semi-flaccid cock roar back to life. But the greedy bastard would have to wait. We were learning our mate.

"I was in jail, facing two years on the inside and probation after that. I didn't want to go through all that and deal with the same techie bullshit when I got out. Earth isn't...it wasn't..." She sighed and stretched her leg forward, tangled it with mine as her hand traced some unknown pattern on my chest. I'd let her write a tome about Earth customs as long as she didn't stop touching me. "Earth wasn't good for me."

Evon came to sit at the bottom of the bed, placing a tray beside him. On it was a plate of sliced fruit, nuts and bread, a glass of water. "Do not fear, mate. What you did on your planet does not affect you here." She looked down the bed to Evon. "You were a prisoner, yes? You broke one of your Earth laws?"

Ah, so that was it. She nodded in confirmation.

"Did you harm anyone?" I asked. She didn't seem to be a cruel person and I doubted the testing would match us to someone with no conscience.

"Of course not. I...I hacked the CEO's private network and published his personal files on the dark web. He was a liar, inflating subscriber numbers and lying about costs. I ruined his chances of selling his business. I cost him millions of dollars. I cost him money," she added when we gave her a funny look about the word "dollars".

"Intriguing," Rager murmured. "What is a dark web?"

"What is hacking?" I asked.

Evon crossed his arms, a frown on his face. "How is this a crime worthy of sending a vulnerable, fragile female to prison when he was the liar? The dishonest one?"

She turned her body so she was on her back and could see all three of us. Her breasts swayed with the motion and it was hard to remain focused. "The dark web is a communications network where you can't be tracked and the government can't control what you do. It's the one place with a free flow of money and information. A lot of people use it, good people and bad. It's become a battle ground. A lot of criminals, spies, and people with secrets operate there. Hackers like me.

"Hacking is using knowledge of computer programming and coding to break the security passwords on someone's computer system and gain access to their information and network. And yes, the big-money players don't want anyone rocking the boat. On Earth, corporations are pretty much in charge of everything, and I definitely rocked the boat." She bit her lip, looking from one of us to another. "You're not upset?"

"Upset that you are very smart? Cunning?" Rager shrugged. Yeah, he wouldn't care all that much. He was the easygoing one and would see her actions as almost humorous. "If they didn't defend themselves well enough to keep you out, then they deserved it."

Yeah, exactly as I thought. I glanced at Evon. He was much more black-and-white. If she committed a crime, then she required a consequence.

He eyed her with his usual ice-blue examination. Debating.

There was no debate for me. What I felt for her, and

what I knew she felt for us in return, mattered more than any crime on another planet.

"What you've done, mate. It's nothing." I swallowed the bitterness that always accompanied these words. "My family is deeply embedded in the VSS, the Viken Sector Separatists. They don't believe in the Coalition and want to take Viken back to a time before we had peace under the three kings, back to civil war."

She frowned. "This planet isn't peaceful?"

"There are no Hive here. None have ever been discovered on the planet. But there are sympathizers with the separatist movement, those who would like to see the current kings and their mate removed from power. They do not want a unified planet. They wish a return to the old ways, to a time where each sector was self-governing and bloodshed was the norm."

"Our queen, Leah, is from Earth. She, too, was matched to three Viken warriors through the Brides Program. To the three kings." Evon offered this truth. "Their daughter, Princess Allayna, is the one true heir. When she becomes queen, she will unite all of Viken forever."

The way her eyes widened in surprise, she hadn't known anything about our planet's history. It seemed she didn't know much of anything about Viken, just as we knew nothing of Earth. I was relieved, for it gave me the opportunity to tell her about the VSS and my family without any preconceived notions on her side. I took a deep breath and blurted out the rest.

"My father and brother are high-ranking members of the VSS. I was to follow in their footsteps, take over as a rebel military leader from my father." I looked down at the dark blanket, then back up at her. "But I didn't. I was caught trying to burn a government building to the ground when I was young and sent to prison. I chose to join the Coalition Fleet instead, and because of this, my father vowed never to speak to me again."

"I'm sorry." She lifted a hand to my jaw and there was no malice in her eyes, no judgment. "That stinks. So, you were all in the Coalition Fleet. Are you are done with that now? I noticed your uniforms. All different colors. What does that mean?"

She was between us naked, not concerned about modesty. I watched her closely to ensure she didn't chill, but I would not have her covered. Neither, I was sure, would the others. I enjoyed seeing her body, breathing in the musky scent of our seed mixed with her arousal.

"We are members of the Viken United Royal Guard now. Our uniform colors represent the Sector where we were born and raised, but the red band around our arms signifies our loyalty to the kings and the Coalition Fleet. This station houses the most important communication system on the planet. We are deployed here to maintain the array and keep it safe. Without the array, we would lose contact with the Fleet and be vulnerable to Hive attack."

Evon added more. "Our transport capabilities would be severely limited, and we would be unable to transport warriors or brides on or off the planet."

"So, where are we?" she asked. "What's it like outside? I have seen nothing of the planet."

Evon stood, went to the window, naked as the day he was born, and pushed a button. The darkening filter was turned off and the view of the frozen landscape filled the entire wall. The brightness of light dancing off snow made me wince.

"Wow." She stood and went over to the window to look outside. Evon moved to stand behind her, to wrap his arms about her. While I wasn't interested in seeing Evon's bare ass, I enjoyed seeing our mate relaxing in his embrace. She was safe. Content. And that was all that mattered to me. Seeing the hard edges around Evon's eyes relax was practically a miracle.

"It's so beautiful," she exclaimed. "It's like the North Pole. Where are Santa and his reindeer?"

"We do not know this Santa. Is he a warrior? And what are reindeer?" Evon asked.

She laughed and the sound made all three of us smile. A rare occurrence indeed. "It's a fairy tale for children about a jolly old man who delivers gifts to children at Christmas. He lives at the North Pole, surrounded by land that looks like this. Completely white, covered with ice and snow." She shivered, then laughed again. "God, just looking at it makes me cold."

"Then I shall warm you." Evon pulled her more tightly to him, completely enfolding her in his arms until she disappeared from my view. "We are in the far north of Viken. This station sits on the tip of the planet, closest to the Coalition Fleet where we have a direct line of sight to their nearest transport and communication station."

"So, this station controls all of Viken's communication with the rest of the universe?"

I moved to sit on the edge of the bed, grabbed a slice of fruit from the plate, and popped it in my mouth. "Yes."

She sighed. "No wonder they sent bad-ass military personnel to guard it."

"Bad-ass?" Rager asked, sitting up so he leaned against the head of the giant bed. "My ass is very good, mate."

Bella began to squirm in Evon's hold. He loosened his grip, let her step back. The bright winter light illuminated her. I couldn't miss the flush that crept from her cheeks and down her neck. Before our eyes, her nipples hardened and she rubbed her thighs together.

"I'm too hot when you hold me like that," she admitted.

I smiled. "Too hot, mate? Don't you mean, aroused?"

She looked to me. "No."

Out of the corner of my eye, I saw Rager nod before rising from the bed to stalk toward her. With the pretty flush on her skin, I'd be right behind him.

She took a step back, then stopped, her arms crossed over her breasts. "Wow. You're right," she admitted. "I'm... god, I'm horny."

I had not heard that word before, but it translated just fine. Especially when she cupped her pussy with one palm, her eyes drifting half closed as she rubbed the soft mound.

"Is this from your seed power? I mean, I like sex and all, and I think you three are the hottest guys I've ever seen, but I've never been like this." She shuddered, caressed her own breast, pushed two of her fingers deep into her feminine heat and the wet sound of our seed filled the room.

I growled, coming up off the bed, my cock hard as a rock, more than ready to ease her.

Evon reached out, but she side-stepped. I expected him to be his bossy self, but he said nothing.

"Never been like what, mate?" Rager asked. I saw him grip his cock, begin to stroke it. I was hard, too, but I didn't reach for my own length. I wanted no touch but hers, right now. Her hand, her mouth, her pussy. I wasn't choosy. Just seeing her slide a finger into her pussy, to know that she was hot for us, made me want to bend her over and fuck her again. Make her scream.

"Like I want to get on my knees and suck all your cocks. Like I need more of that seed." She moaned, then closed her eyes, pumping her fingers in and out of her pussy as we all watched, mesmerized. "Like I'm going insane."

Rager moved closer and stood beside Evon. "Not insane. You're our mate and you desire us."

"Desire you?" she asked, her eyes becoming wild. "I want to *devour* you."

"Here you go, mate," Rager said as he held the base of his cock so it pointed directly at Bella.

Evon's cock was just as hard, but he did nothing, just kept his hands at his sides, remaining silent.

"Don't you want to boss me around?" she asked, looking to Evon. Gods, she knew us so well already.

Evon shook his head. "This time you take what you want."

Perhaps that was no different than issuing another order, for he was commanding her to do whatever she wished. He watched her intently, eager to see what she would choose to do now that she was in control. I waited as well, barely able to breathe. Would she drop to her knees and take one of us deep into her mouth? Would she leap into Rager's arms and impale herself on his hard length, beg Evon to take her from behind? Would she stand between them and work both of them with her hands as I watched?

Every possibility raced through my mind, and I wanted to see them all.

She moved then, taking the few steps that separated them and falling to her knees so she was directly before their bobbing cocks. She didn't take them in her mouth, instead gripped the base of each one in her small hands. As she did so, Rager's and Evon's hips bucked, but she turned her head to me. "I need you, too."

I didn't wait for a second invitation. Fuck, no. If she was going to suck all three of us off, to fill her belly up with our cum, to ensure she was completely under the spell of seed power, then I wasn't going to deny her. Gods knew, I could deny her nothing already.

I went to join them, but the door chime stalled me.

I looked to Rager and Evon, whose cocks were being stroked by our mate's fists. She was licking her lips, her gaze meeting mine. I knew what she intended as she used her tongue to tease me, stroking her bottom lip in blatant invitation. My mate was eager to swallow my cock—and there was someone at the damn door?

I ignored it. We had our mate. We were on leave. We didn't need to answer the fucking door. I stepped right up to Bella so my cock brushed against her cheek, a small smudge of my seed left there as she licked the broad crown.

She moaned as the small dose of seed power hit her. I groaned at the feel of her tongue swirling over me. I vaguely heard the door chime again, but she'd licked down the underside of my cock to take one of my balls in her mouth.

"Fuck," I growled as my eyes rolled back in my head.

I heard a commotion, heard Evon say something, then other voices, but I didn't give a fuck. I'd never had my balls in my mate's mouth before and I was going to shoot my load all over her face if she didn't swallow me down.

"Liam Chyron of Sector 1," someone bellowed.

I felt Rager's hand on my shoulder, heard his words. "Step back and protect Bella. We have company."

Bella's mouth was gone. Only then did I open my eyes

and groan. She wasn't on her knees before me any longer. My balls ached. It was then the needy haze cleared. I watched as Rager stepped between us and the door. Evon wrapped Bella in a blanket, covering her from neck to ankle.

"Liam Chyron of Sector 1."

I spun about, saw the station commander standing in the doorway, surrounded by three guards. Their gazes flicked over the four of us, what we'd been doing—or about to do—quite obvious. Other than them seeing Bella on her knees naked, I didn't give a fuck.

Rager held out his hands to halt their movement. He was huge, and mean as hell when riled, and everyone knew it. The guards stopped dead in their tracks, trying to look everywhere but at our raging hard-ons. I wasn't ashamed of my desire for my mate. I'd had my mate's tongue on my damn balls and they'd interrupted.

We formed a solid wall between the guards and Bella, all three of us naked and ready to fight to the death to protect our mate.

"What is the meaning of this, Commander?" Evon demanded.

Bella tried to peek over my shoulder, but I wrapped my arm around her and gently pushed her to stand behind me. This was strange, to say the least. They'd broken into our private quarters, armed and were now pointing weapons at three members of the Royal Guard. Something terrible was going on here, and until I knew what, I didn't want her exposed to these men who could turn out to be our enemies.

The commander nodded his head to Evon in a show of respect. We'd served under him for several years now. "My apologies, gentlemen, for interrupting your private time with your new mate."

"Then why are you here? And why did you break into our quarters?" Rager's question was more growl than actual words, his fists clenching and unclenching at his sides.

"We are here for Liam." His gaze turned to me, and all three of his companions shifted so that their weapons pointed at my chest. None too gently, I used my other arm to nudge Bella over to stand behind Rager. That was a lot of firepower aimed my way, and I would not risk her being caught in the fire.

"What?" I growled, my hands in fists. "I'm right here. What do you want? What is the meaning of this?"

The commander looked me dead in the eye. "You're under arrest for treason."

6

Watching three brutish guards escort Liam from our bedroom was like a blow to the solar plexus. One moment I'd been in bliss, surrounded by my new mates, eager to take them into my mouth and bring each of them pleasure. I'd felt powerful and beautiful at the same time, something I'd never experienced before. And now?

Now I wanted to take on the three guards dressed in black and scream.

Had Liam done something wrong? What had I gotten myself into? Was my mate a traitor? A criminal? Had I walked out of the frying pan and into the fire, choosing to leave Earth behind? My conviction had been vacated when I became an Interstellar Bride, but would I be matched to a criminal because I'd been one myself?

Doubts crept into my mind, slowly, like a dark sludge

suffocating my joy. The glow of our mating faded quickly, leaving me cold and shivering even as Evon and Rager stood between me and the others, a living, breathing wall. Nothing was getting through them. I knew that. And that knowledge was the only thing keeping me on my feet as this ice-covered world ripped the rug out from under me.

Evon and the commander faced one another in silence as Liam walked silently between the others.

"There has been a mistake," Rager insisted.

"I'm afraid not." The commander was unapologetic. Even his eyes were empty, resigned. "Liam's security codes were used to transport stolen weapons and communications equipment to Sector 1."

"That's impossible." Evon shook his head, even as he took a step back. I couldn't see his face, but I could hear the shock in his voice.

Liam was gone, vanished into the hallway with the three guards. They hadn't even allowed him to put on his clothes. No, they were going to parade him through the halls to somewhere—jail?—like a savage, naked and exposed. And that really made me want to kick this guy in the balls.

"The judicial hearing is scheduled for two hours from now. If you're going to prove him innocent, I'd hurry." With that, the commander spun on his heel and left me alone with Rager and Evon.

The moment the door slid closed behind the intruders, Evon turned to face us, his cool mask slipping away to reveal pure rage. His eyes, usually icy blue, were filled with heat now, but a very cold heat. "He didn't do this, Bella. I promise you."

Rager agreed with a quick nod. "It's impossible. Liam is ours. He's fought at our sides against the Hive, saved both our lives. There is no way he betrayed Viken." He pulled me into his arms, as much, I felt, to reassure himself as to comfort me.

"But..." I hated to play devil's advocate, but I seemed to be the only one with a level head at the moment. Which wasn't saying much, considering my mental state was shaky at best. The seed power lingered, but it turned to a fierce protectiveness for Liam, even while my mind wondered of his innocence. No, he was innocent. My body, my mind, ached from the confusion. "What about his family? Their ties to the VSS? The bad guys, right? Are you sure?"

Evon turned my head from Rager's chest and kissed me hard and fast. Not long enough. A punishment. "I will forgive this line of questioning once, Bella, because you are new here. You do not know what we know. You have not seen what we've seen. You do not fully know us or perhaps the extent of evil of the Hive. But I vow to you on my life, more, on my honor, Liam would never betray us."

It was hard to argue with the unbreakable steely resolve in his gaze. He believed what he was saying. So, I had a choice to make. If I refuted him now, I'd be betraying not just Liam, but Evon as well. "All right," I said. I was willing to trust in the match, in them. "So, if Liam is innocent, who used his security codes?"

Part of me couldn't believe we were even having this conversation. Hadn't I just been on Earth talking about programming, hacking, identity theft? Hadn't I just spent time in a jail cell for doing just that? "I can't believe you guys don't have this stuff on lock-down. For an advanced race who can transport living beings clear across the universe, this seems ridiculous."

I turned and sat on the edge of the bed as my mates scrambled into their uniforms.

"The hearing will begin in two hours." Rager moved quickly, already fully dressed in his dark gray uniform. He was magnificent, my mate, and the tight fit of his uniform only emphasized the width of his shoulders, the strength of his chest. He was power personified, and he was mine.

"We will begin at the transport station. Track the real traitor from there. I don't care who we have to pound into dust to get answers." Evon's voice was smooth and even, despite the fact that his words were not.

"I'm going, too." I stood up and walked to the drawer that Rager had opened in the wall, hoping to find something for me to wear besides the gauzy gown I'd worn when I arrived. Inside were more clothing items. I pulled out a pair of pants and held them up to my frame. "You have a belt?" If I used a belt, I might be able to strap the leather under my arms and wear the things like a jumper. It would be baggy, but I couldn't walk around wearing a nightgown and nothing beneath.

"No, mate. You will stay here." Evon wasn't even looking at me, and Rager was waiting by the door, impatient to be off.

What?

"Summon Thalia. She can watch over our mate." Rager grinned at me then, finding obvious humor in my proposed use of his clothes. I knew I looked ridiculous, but I had no idea where to find something that fit.

Evon glanced up at me and froze, the corners of his eyes creasing despite the fact that he didn't smile. He helped me out of my oversized pants so I was bare once again, went and picked up the gown they'd stripped from me and helped me back into it. "For now, wear this. I enjoy knowing you are bare beneath for me. You must remain here, Bella. Safe. I will summon Thalia, my sister. She is stationed here as well. She will protect you in our absence."

"No." I shook my head, but my mates weren't listening. Evon walked to me and took my face in his huge hands. His skin was calloused, but warm. His touch was gentle.

"We need to know you are safe, mate. And you need food. Rest. My sister is a trusted member of the guard. She served four years in the Coalition Fleet. She will allow no harm to come to you until our return."

His kiss melted me to my toes, and before I could argue, Rager took his place. By the time he was done with me, I was swaying on my feet in a daze.

Damn, my mates could kiss the wits right out of me.

The door slid closed behind them and I dropped onto the bed to nibble on the fruit and cheese they'd left behind. There was enough food for a small army, or at least one average-size human and three hulking warriors. By the time I was full, a chime sounded at the door.

Energy renewed, I jumped to my feet and opened the door. A tall woman with long golden hair and Evon's eyes stared down at me. She was close to six-foot tall, and beautiful.

She bowed at the waist, her black uniform and red arm band clearly marking her as a member of the same sector as her brother. But there was no doubt they were related. I would have recognized that no-nonsense, ice-blue gaze anywhere. "Lady Bella. I am Thalia. Your new sister."

My new sister. When I chose to be matched, I expected a mate. I'd gotten three. I never imagined they'd have family, that, by extension, I would have a sister or brother, nieces or nephews. In-laws. It seemed weird, but I was pleased. I wasn't alone.

I stepped back. "Please, come in." I carried the tray of food to the small side table in the living area as the door slid closed behind her. "I have plenty of food, if you're hungry."

She shook her head and remained standing near the door. "Welcome to Viken, sister. I am very happy that my brother has found a mate, even if he is foolish enough to share you with the others."

That was odd, but then, I didn't know everything about this planet. Hell, I knew almost nothing. "Why do they do that? Three men and one woman? Doesn't that mess up the ratios for the rest of you?" I hadn't meant it to sound cold, but Thalia's shoulders stiffened.

"The three kings began a new tradition, one warrior from each sector and a shared mate. The idea was to unify the sectors over time, create a new generation of warriors who looked at Viken as one united planet."

Children of fathers from the three sectors. They would be...sector-less and could unify the planet. My mind was doing the math, and it didn't add up. "But, by that logic, aren't there two women on Viken who can't find a mate for every Interstellar Bride?"

"No. Every year Viken sends an equal number of women and men to serve the Coalition, either as brides or warriors for the Fleet. Not all planets send this many brides. Three of four Viken warriors return. None of the brides return, as they are matched and settle elsewhere. As a result, there are fewer women here for them to choose as mates once they return from the war."

"Oh." That was sad. They fought in the war, suffered,

killed, and when they returned there were no women to choose as mates?

"That is why, centuries ago, the leaders of Prillon Prime insisted on creation of the Interstellar Brides Program. Initially, it was meant to unify planets, create bonds where none existed."

"Political alliances," I muttered. Suddenly, the whole thing made a lot more sense. It was like the royals of Europe in the past, rather than go to war with a country, they just married off their children, forged new treaties, made babies that both countries considered royal heirs. That was how centuries of war between Scotland and England finally came to an end.

"Yes. The Prime believed the Coalition would be more cohesive, more likely to survive as a united front to battle the Hive threat if warriors took brides from other worlds."

I studied her. Her long hair was pulled back into an intricate braid that pressed tightly to her head and made her look somewhat severe. The weapon strapped to her side didn't lessen the effect. She watched me with a mix of curiosity and disapproval in her eyes.

"So, you're happy your brother has a mate, but you disapprove of him following the new custom? One woman with three mates."

She shrugged. "I mean no offense, Bella. While you are only the third bride from Earth, our new queen is from your world. She is very beautiful, with dark red hair and a very feminine form. Many of the warriors have had their heads turned by her beauty, and now desire a bride from Earth."

Ahhh. Realization was dawning. "And the warrior you desire?"

Her fair skin flushed instantly and she turned away to

stare out at the icy tundra still visible along the far wall. "I have no desire other than to serve."

Liar. But I wasn't a bitch, so I let her have her secrets. Knowing each other for five minutes wasn't long enough for her to bare her soul. Looked like me and the sister-in-law weren't going to be besties anytime soon. I could live with that. Civil was good enough for now. "Okay. Well, I have a desire."

She turned back to face me, a question in her eyes.

"I want some clothes. Underwear. Something I can wear in public where my mates won't rip other warriors' heads off. My nipples are poking out, for god's sake. And then I want to go to Liam's hearing. I'm not sitting in this room like a pet while they decide his fate."

Her next words surprised me. So did the determination in her eyes. "Agreed."

Wow. That had been a lot easier than I'd thought it would be. She walked to the far wall and opened a drawer I hadn't seen and pulled out a cream-colored set of clothing. Why hadn't Evon just grabbed those for me instead of the dang nightgown dress? That was right, he liked to know I was bare. The fact I was turned on by the idea only empowered me to grab the other clothing. If I was going out in public, I didn't want to risk the chance of wanting to climb him—or my other mates—like a wild monkey. "This is standard issue for civilians. Put it on."

She handed me the pile. It was soft, like cashmere, and lined with the finest fur. I imagined it would be warm and extremely comfortable. But I was covered in sex and sweat and interstellar transport dust.

"Is there a bathtub around here? Or a shower?"

She pointed to a door in the far wall as she walked to the

tray of food, grabbed a piece of the fruit and nibbled. She waved her hand. "Be quick, Bella of Earth. I don't want to miss anything. And Evon might need me."

I grabbed the new clothes and dashed to the bathroom, relieved to find a fairly self-explanatory setup. I'd feel like an idiot if I had to ask Thalia for help in working a bathtub. As the hot water washed away the last few hours, I had to wonder what kind of hell the beautiful Thalia had endured, why she was so jaded about me and my warriors, and which warrior here had broken her heart.

ager

WHEN EVON AND I ARRIVED AT THE CIVIL SERVICES CENTER for the judicial hearing, I had expected the usual panel of five leaders to preside. What I hadn't expected was Evon's father to be among the five, or his brother to be seated in the audience. Evon obviously hadn't anticipated them either, for he stopped just inside the doorway and I bumped into his back. Then I saw the direction of his gaze and I stifled a curse.

While Evon was my closest of friends—along with Liam —he was ruled by rules, codes of conduct, honor. He was unbending. Evon's family had served the planet for centuries, believed that nothing was more important than serving with honor. Always had. He was uptight, laser-focused and that made him a good leader. Exceptional, in fact, and that trait had brought all of us back from the front lines alive. It also made him a very dominant lover, which Bella quickly discovered.

But years of companionship, of trust between the three of us, had softened some of Evon's very hard edges. It was possible I may have even seen a smile crack his lips when he was looking at Bella earlier. She was good for all of us, but especially him. If anyone could calm him, offer him a semblance of peace, it would be her.

But Evon's father, Commander Tyrell? He was so damned uptight he shit Viken ore. His son—his *other* son, Dravon—was just as bad. He'd followed in his father's footsteps in civil command and had stayed solely on Viken. Unlike Evon, who went into the Coalition Fleet and became one of the fighters serving on a Prillon battleship. We'd fought the fucking Hive while his father and brother had remained much closer to home. Evon and his sister, Thalia, had been off saving the universe while his bad-tempered father and brother remained to protect the home front.

They were all noble, their family history only proved Evon's family was loyal to the core. They believed in Viken, served Viken, even commanded large sections of it. Having Evon serving as a high-ranking officer in the IQC only added to the Tyrell family's influence on the planet.

Having Evon's father, Commander Tyrell, seated on the panel meant Liam was fucked. There was no gray area for that man, for that family. I had no idea what they would accuse Liam of doing, but if there was a shred of doubt, there would be no mercy in the commander's decision. I clenched and unclenched my fists, my mind racing with possibilities.

The penalty for treason was death.

And there was no way they were taking Liam without a

fight. He was innocent. I knew it for a fact, would stake my life on it.

I watched as Evon nodded to his father and brother in turn before taking a seat amongst the ten or so before the panel. A few members of the IQC community were present, perhaps because they were waiting for someone else to appear once Liam's hearing was over.

Liam entered, two guards flanking him. Thankfully, they'd given him some damn clothes. Why they took him away stark naked, I had no idea. They positioned him to the side of the room, remaining standing as the charges were read. He wore the simple cream-colored clothing of a civilian. I had rarely seen him in anything but his brown uniform. The light color, the lack of a red armband, was strange to my eyes.

Liam stood tall, his shoulders squared and his eyes blazed with defiance. There was no mistaking the warrior's stance, despite the clothing they'd forced him to wear as a punishment. What kind of game were they playing? Was he not still a member of the Royal Guard?

The female Viken on the far left of the panel stood. She wore a brown uniform as a representative from Sector 1. "Liam Chyron of Sector 1," she began. She lifted her dark eyes from the tablet in her hand, looked at my friend with serious intent. "The charges that have brought you before this panel are: Conspiracy, smuggling of illegal goods, stealing royal property, stealing Coalition property, illegal weapons transport, unauthorized use of mobile transport pads, treason against the crowned kings of Viken, and murder."

She read the charges like they were nothing more than a shopping list, but when she lifted her gaze to his, her look alone was enough to strike a lesser man down. "These are very serious charges, sir. How would you address the charges against you?"

While I didn't hear the door slide open behind me, I knew Bella had entered the room. I *sensed* her. A moment later her sweet scent reached me and Evon stiffened next to me. The hair on the back of my neck stood on end and my cock lengthened and hardened beneath my uniform pants. I stood, then turned. Evon followed. Someone behind us cleared their throat.

"What is the meaning of this disruption?"

I ignored the voice and took Bella's hand, met her dark eyes, which sparked with irritation. Perhaps she was annoyed with her mates for leaving her behind. But she was not the only one irritated. She should not be here. But my mate was innocent in this. I aimed my anger at Evon's sister, Thalia, who accompanied her. While Bella had only been on the planet for a few hours, Thalia should know better than to interrupt a military judicial hearing.

"My apologies, Commander," Liam said. I saw him out of the corner of my eye and his fists were clenched at his sides. Yeah, he was pissed, too. "This is Bella, of Earth, my mate, and she has come to witness the proceedings."

What else could he say? He wasn't in a position to argue, only pacify.

"I was not aware you took a mate." I glanced up, saw that it was Evon's father who spoke. He looked at her, his eyes narrowed. "Is this true, Bella? Is Liam Chyron your mate?"

On the spot, Bella looked him in eye and lifted her chin. She refused both Evon's and my touch, choosing to hold her hands loosely before her as she addressed the commander. "Yes. I arrived several hours ago. I am an Interstellar Bride,

84

sent from Earth. I have been matched to Liam, Rager, and Evon."

Evon's brother spun about in his chair and he stared at Bella. I pulled her to a chair and we sat, Evon on her other side.

Bella kept her head up and looked quite like the queen. Not in coloring, for she didn't have the bright red hair, but certainly in mannerisms. Bella wasn't going to cower before this panel, nor her new father and brother-in-law. They were formidable; that was why they held such lofty roles.

"Yet I assume she is not yet claimed," Evon's brother clarified.

I watched as Evon's jaw clenched and I wondered if his back molars might crack. While he was not removed from his family as Liam was from his, they had strong beliefs. They stood for a unified Viken with as powerful a conviction as Liam's believed in the VSS. But his family was not open and friendly, easygoing and loving as mine was. My childhood in Sector 3 was idyllic without any of the pressure put upon my friends.

The fact that Dravon stated that Bella had yet to be officially claimed proved it. Yes, she was our mate, but until we'd claimed her—all three of us fucking and filling her at the same time—the bond could be broken. She could be sent to another. It was a sharp twist of a ruthless blade, pointing out this fact, this weakness and vulnerability to his own brother.

The fucker. I was the damn pacifist among the three of us, but right now, I hated Evon's brother. He was an asshole that needed to be knocked down a few pegs.

Even Bella, who knew nothing about our ways, picked up on the wording, the interplay between siblings. Her back was ramrod straight and her eyes were narrowed. I put a hand on her thigh, felt it tense, but she quickly relaxed.

It was then I realized she wasn't wearing that filmy white gown she transported in, instead warm clothing that covered her body modestly. Thank fuck Thalia had helped her. No doubt she would have come to this hearing in just a wrap Evon had draped over her. Would our Bella have arrived with her lush breasts and hard nipples obvious for everyone to see? I might be the calm one of our new family, but I would have had her over my shoulder and out of the room before she put her ass in a chair.

"The charges against me are severe. As I am innocent, I demand to know on what grounds you lay these claims at my feet," Liam said, returning the conversation back to the situation at hand. His voice was calm, but as his friend I recognized his tenseness, that he was tightly coiled from this, from having Bella in the room. His stance was more Evon than Liam.

"You should be ashamed of yourself," the panel member from Sector 1 added. "Your family has caused enough trouble through the years, but even your father has not resorted to murder."

She was wrong, but the knowledge Liam had shared with me in the past was not pertinent today. Liam's father was a killer, a cold-blooded, calculating murderer who rationalized every evil act with his fanatical belief in separatist politics.

"Murder?" Liam asked, his voice loud. "I am no murderer. I served long years in the Coalition Fleet, defending this planet. I have sworn an oath to the three kings, am a member of the Royal Guard, and have taken a mate shared by three sectors to unify the planet. I am innocent of your claims."

Bella took my hand, gripped it tight.

Murder?

"A technician in the transport center was killed by an ion blast to the heart. Doctors estimate his time of death to be five minutes prior to the transport of stolen goods."

Liam shook his head. "I had nothing to do with this. Why am I here?"

"Your security codes were used to initiate the transport and bypass IQC security protocols."

Shit. The use of Liam's codes was shocking. No one shared codes. They were implanted in special quantum crystals just under the skin of our wrists. There was no sharing, no faking the codes. They were assigned randomly and programmed by the Coalition's computer system.

The look on Liam's face was half anger, half stunned. He'd only killed Hive and they were the enemy. And using his security code? Short of cutting off his arm or dragging him to a control station, no one could use it. Hell, no one would even know what it was. Liam didn't even know what it was, a randomized sequence of over two hundred letters, symbols and forms made up from pieces of all the languages in the Interstellar Coalition. It was impossible to break.

"That's impossible," Liam began. "Based on your statement, you have an exact time for this incident. When did this occur?"

"Twenty-two fifty-three," another member of the panel said, his head down as if reading the fact from his tablet.

That was last night. Fairly late. Bella hadn't arrived yet. Hell, I hadn't even been tested yet. Evon's testing had been first, yesterday morning. Liam's had been just after dinner, several hours before the incident in question.

I heard Evon swear under his breath. We must both be thinking the same thing. Liam was most likely alone in his own quarters then. We only received access to the Mated Family Quarters this morning after we were matched.

"Do you have an alibi for this time?" Commander Tyrell asked.

I swore I saw Liam blush. "I was alone in my quarters. I'd completed my testing for the Interstellar Brides Program at the medical station and returned to my quarters. Have any of you been tested for a match?" he asked the panel.

I knew Evon's father was mated, obviously, but hadn't been matched. All of the others shook their heads. Either they weren't mated at all, or had found their mate without the assistance of the Brides Program.

"It is grueling and I spent time in the shower before I fell asleep," Liam finished.

Grueling? It was a sex dream. An epic sex dream and I'd come like an overeager youth. Thankfully, I hadn't come in my pants and it had been easy to laugh off my hard-on to the doctor who facilitated the test. That was just the way I was. Surely the doctor had seen it all before. I'd wanted to jerk off, to ease the pressure after the testing, but we'd been immediately matched. I could well imagine the sexual frustration. I was not surprised that Liam needed to find relief by taking himself in hand in the shower.

Was that why he blushed? He had no interest in telling the panel he was masturbating while someone was being murdered. It wouldn't bode well for a guard of his standing to admit it, even though all of the males in the panel had surely taken themselves in hand before. Surely the female from Sector 1 got herself off a time or two.

"Your personal security code was used. That is strong enough evidence to require a formal trial," the commander said.

"It's not strong evidence," Bella said, popping to her feet. "Anyone can use someone else's code to hack into a system."

Evon took hold of her arm and tried to tug her back down, but she would have none of it, twisting her arm in his grip and pulling as hard as she could.

"Silence," Commander Tyrell tilted his head, his gaze gone from severe to angry.

Bella didn't sit down. Nor did she stop talking. "I don't care how advanced you think your cyber security is, even if someone can't break his code, they can hack the system that created it. There is always a back door, always a way in. Someone using Liam's code proves nothing."

"The codes have never been broken," the woman from Sector 1 insisted.

"I can break them." Bella's declaration brought the room to sudden silence.

The commander rose to his feet, a very clear threat in his eyes. I rose to stand next to her as Evon did the same.

"My mate is a highly skilled computational technician," Liam offered. "She is well versed in this type of activity."

Meaning, she was a hacker and could break into systems.

"I can prove it," she said. "I can prove Liam is innocent and that you have a very serious problem in your security system."

Evon's father arched a silvery brow. "You're from Earth?"

"Yes."

"Such a primitive planet. How do you think you can infiltrate Coalition systems?"

She crossed her arms, but focused on the woman from Sector 1, or rather, on the tablet she carried.

"Is that tablet linked to the rest of the system?" she asked.

"Yes."

"If I may use that, I can show you."

The other members of the panel were looking to Commander Tyrell, not at Liam.

Liam looked as if he were about to fling Bella over his shoulder and run off with her.

Evon was as still and fucking stiff as a statue.

The commander remained silent for a moment, then nodded. The woman held out her tablet. Bella looked up at me, determination in her eyes. I followed her up to the raised dais where she took the proffered tablet.

Her head lowered as her fingers flew over the flat screen. "I assume the video or whatever visual evidence you should have had from the transport room doesn't exist."

I hadn't thought of that. Whomever did murder the poor technician and transported the stolen goods, they would have appeared on the security vids. If they erased all video evidence, only the security access code would connect someone to the crime. Liam.

Bella didn't wait for a reply, for she knew the answer.

"You are Evon's father and have three other children. Your name is Bywen Alixor Tyrell. You were born in Sector 2 to a widow named Janza, your father Alix having died in the Hive wars serving *Battleship Zakar*, Sector 17, before you were born. You broke your left ring finger when you were twelve and this is why you only purchased a ring for your mate when you claimed her, never acquiring one for yourself." Bella kept her eyes on the tablet as she spoke. "Ah, that's so sweet. Earth marriages have rings, too. Let's see...your residence in Viken United has had deliveries for some kind of food item I've never heard of. Pornice? Is that it?"

Whispers came from the panel and I saw that the commander's face was turning a ruddy red. She was learning more than she should while proving her point. Pornice was a rich delicacy imported from Prillon Prime. It was fattening and famously expensive. Only rich snobs requested it on Viken. But Bella wouldn't know that and pointing it out now would only come across as obnoxious.

"Let's see. That's all very interesting, but let's dig a little deeper." Her fingers flew over the tablet, almost faster than I could see, her eyes darting rapidly, analyzing and adapting to what she saw. I was in awe. Her mind was working faster than any I'd ever seen. When a sly grin tilted the corner of her lip, I braced myself for worse than Pornice. "I see you are a member of a club called Trinity in Central City, which isn't far from here. You've been a Master there for twenty years and are marked with a three-headed serpent on the inside of your wrist. Your commanding officer made note of it in your file, but next to it he wrote something about the habit not affecting your combat skills? Whatever this 'habit' is?" She shrugged, her fingers, flying over the pad again. "Your mate also belongs to the club. Her name is—"

"Enough!" It wasn't the commander who shouted, but Dravon.

Evon had paled, his face unmoving, hard as granite. Trinity was a members-only sex establishment in the largest city on the northern continent. That meant that Evon's father was a Master-level Dominant with years of training. I hid a grin. Seemed our Evon came by the tendency quite naturally.

Nothing Bella had said was a matter of planet-wide security, but the commander was embarrassed. As a Master Dominant, he would have participated in a wide variety of sex acts, hopefully with Evon's mother, although it was known that members often swapped sexual partners.

Bella lifted her head then. "I can go on. Give me access to a fully functional communications station here, and I bet I can hack the security access codes of every member of this station." Her head tilted to the side, and I realized she was talking more to herself than anyone else in the room. "Or swap them. If no one knows who's who, a switch might be easier than a full hack."

"It appears my mate has proven her point." Liam's crisp words were spoken quickly, to keep the panel and everyone off the tidbits learned about one of Viken's highest leaders. "I am quite sure the private personnel file of our esteemed commander was not without protection."

The Sector 1 panel member spoke. "It does seem as if the information your mate has shared was confidential enough for me to have reasonable doubt as to the use of your access code." She looked to the others. "Do you agree?"

Three of them nodded and she waited for Commander Tyrell's ruling. While his was not necessary; if he disagreed, he would still be outnumbered four to one in favor of Liam's release.

He stared at Bella, then Evon. My friend put a hand on her shoulder.

"I am convinced we need to investigate this matter further," the commander said. "Release him, but he is not to leave the station."

"Yes, sir." The guard nearest Liam removed the manacles from his wrists, as Bella took a small hop in her excitement and pulled me into her in celebration. I was proud of our new mate, and knew Evon was as well. His arms came around her, here, on full display of his family. But Evon's brother rose, icy anger settled over him like a cloud, making his eyes cold, hard points glittering in his flushed face.

"How dare you?" He was walking toward us, toward Evon. "How dare you do this, brother?"

Evon turned and pushed Bella behind him before turning to face his brother. Face-to-face, they were nearly mirror images of one another. Same golden hair, same height and build, but Dravon was five years younger and spoiled. Hot-headed. He'd not been hardened by battle as Evon had. As I had. He was, in my mind, still a child. An impulsive, rude little boy who needed his ass kicked.

"Careful, Dravon."

"Or what?" Dravon pushed Evon in the chest, going nose to nose with his older brother. "A few hours with your cock buried in your mate's wet pussy and you lose your mind? We all know Liam is guilty. His family bleeds for the VSS, always has. I can't believe you're so stupid as to believe him." Dravon glanced at me, at Bella, then back at Evon. "He's a liar and a murderer, and I'm going to make sure he pays for what he did."

The young fool pushed Evon again, but I knew my friend, knew he would never dishonor his family as Dravon did now. The little bastard needed to be put in his place, but Evon would not be the one to do it.

I, however, had no such inhibitions. And I didn't like him talking about Bella. She was mine. And her hot, wet pussy? That was fucking mine, too.

Liam shouted at me to stop, but it was too late.

With a shout of laughter, I pulled back and then punched the cocky little bastard right in the face.

He flew back, dead weight when he hit the floor. Hard.

Not hard enough.

"Gods be damned, Rager!" Liam yelled at me, but I was watching Dravon twist and roll on the floor, coming back to himself. The commander shouted at the guards to take me down, but I didn't care. No, I wanted to strike him again for his disrespect of both my friend and my mate.

"Stay down, you arrogant little ass. How dare you speak to Evon that way?" I bellowed the last. "And never speak of my mate again or I will pound you into dust."

I took a step toward him, but small, soft hands wrapped around my elbow, pulling me back.

"Rager! Stop!" Bella's voice was like a chime in my mind, waking me up. I glanced around to see four guards with ion blasters pointed at my chest.

von

RAGER WAS ENRAGED, OUT OF CONTROL. I KNEW HIM TO BE Viken, but I had to wonder if he were part Atlan beast. When he became angry, it was as if he were possessed by some inner animal. That he protected me...

Out of the corner of my eye I saw Liam move toward him, but Bella, our fearless mate, wrapped her hands around Rager's arm.

I remained motionless, ready to move quickly should he fail to regain control. But Bella's touch, or perhaps her voice, snapped him back to himself. He still towered over Dravon, who remained sprawled on the floor. Blood seeped from my brother's nose to his upper lip and he raised his arm to wipe the liquid away on his sleeve.

"Arrest this man," Dravon shouted.

Two of the four guards surrounding us lowered their

weapons and took a step forward. I raised my hand and stepped in front of Rager and our mate. "No. You deserved worse, brother."

My brother scowled at me from his position on the floor as Thalia stepped out from where she'd been sitting and helped him back up. The moment his feet were solidly beneath him, he shrugged her off as if her touch burned. She stood to the side, glancing between our brother and Rager, her heart in her eyes.

I'd known for long months she wanted Rager for her own. Our decision to follow the new way, the kings' way, and share a bride had killed her fragile hope. But she was hard, a true soldier, unlike our spoiled little brother. She didn't act on her desires, kept them to herself, but I knew her well and her looks betrayed her. At least to me.

When the commander, our father, raised his hand, silence descended and I could hear nothing but my own racing heartbeat and Dravon's ragged breathing.

"Lower your weapons."

The guards did as he bid and stepped back. Bella crossed her arms over her chest, tapping her foot, and raised a brow at our father. The vision of our defiant little mate staring down one of the most powerful commanders of Viken would be burned into my memory for all time. Our beautiful Bella. Her courage made my cock hard and all I could think about for long seconds was grabbing her by the hair, shoving her up against the wall and burying myself balls deep until my seed power conquered her body, made her melt in my arms. Surrender. Although she was passionate enough I knew the seed power wasn't really needed. She desired us enough without it. I wanted all that fiery intelligence, the steel in her spine, and I wanted her to bend in submission to me. To *give* it to me like the most precious gift.

Hard as iron, my cock throbbed and I had to swallow hard, take a deep breath and close my eyes to force the image from my mind as my father continued.

"Evon, your brother is correct. You know of the Chyron family's link to the VSS. How can you believe in Liam Chyron's innocence with such clear and damning evidence?" He inclined his chin to Bella, but he wasn't finished. "I know your mate claims to be able to prove otherwise, and she's certainly made an attempt to sway us." Sway? She'd exposed some of his most personal secrets to a judicial panel. I tried not to roll my eyes at my father's ability to be ever the diplomat. "The panel has agreed to allow you to try, Bella of Earth."

He put an emphasis on the word "try" as if he knew Liam to be guilty and there would be no evidence otherwise.

Bella nodded, her chin lifted, her gaze direct. Most would cower and placate my father. Not Bella. "Tomorrow."

"Tomorrow," the commander agreed, then looked to me. "Tomorrow you will have to make a choice, son. When your mate is unable to prove her claims, Liam will be found guilty. And he will be executed."

"No." I refused to believe Liam was responsible. I *knew* him not to be. I had no proof, but I didn't need it. I knew Liam.

"He's a traitor." Dravon wiped the blood from his face once more, smearing the red liquid over his cheek as he continued to bleed, and suddenly I wished Rager had struck him harder. Knocked him out. The stubborn little fool. "If you take his side, Evon, if you side with a traitor, you will no longer be my brother."

Thalia gasped, but my father said nothing and I knew, with a sinking feeling in my gut, that he felt the same. I saw it in his eyes. He was waiting for me to step away from my mate, from my warrior brothers who would ultimately claim Bella together. For them. For a stilted version of patriotism. For a blindness that would drive a wedge in our family.

Liam and Rager turned to me. Rager's expression was filled with annoyed disbelief. He'd never understood what it meant to belong to my family, the honor and the expectations. But Liam knew. All too well, for he'd defied his father, been disowned. He'd walked alone for many years and only now, in this moment, did I fully understand the price he'd paid. The deep sense of loss. He mourned something that was still alive.

Liam shook his head at me, the move nearly imperceptible. And that was the only reminder I needed. Even now, Liam protected me, protected our new family. He expected me to turn my back on him as his own father had, his siblings, even his mother. He wanted Rager and me to keep Bella, to make her ours. To keep the connection to my family.

Not today. No fucking way.

"Liam is innocent," I said, holding my brother's gaze. "I would stake my life on his loyalty. He would never betray us." I took a step toward my brother, who wisely backed away. He'd never seen me this angry, the rage like ice in my veins. "If you speak ill of my family again, Dravon, it will be you who are no longer my blood."

"Enough!" My father bellowed that one word and I turned to find his eyes blazing with frustration. "The truth will be revealed soon enough." He looked at Bella. "Tomorrow. You have until tomorrow."

"Fine." Bella slipped her hand into Rager's, but looked between Liam and me. "Can we go now?"

"Yes." I settled my hand on Thalia's shoulder in thanks and her eyes met mine, the familiar blue dark with a tempest of emotion I had no hope of unraveling. "Thank you, little sister."

When she remained silent, her gaze drifting between the three men of her family who were all clearly at odds, I motioned to Liam. "Let's go, Liam, and help our mate prove your innocence."

I wasn't sure where Thalia's alliance rested. I would not question her about it. It wasn't important. Proving Liam's innocence was. I knew my family was lost to me now. Whether she was among those who would consider me a disgrace, I would have to wait and see.

Rager led Bella out the door with Liam falling in behind. I watched the soft sway of her hips beneath the cream pants, the trim shirt. While she was small like an Earth female, she looked Viken now. With our seed in her belly, the Viken clothing covering her lush curves, she was ours more than ever. I wanted to touch her, feel her, breathe in her scent to remind myself of that. She was ours. I walked at the back, as far away from Bella as I could get, afraid I'd give in and take her here, in the hall. I'd never been more desperate to claim a woman, to put my mark on her soul, as I was with our brave little human. Especially now, risking the consequences of a judicial panel for interrupting, the disrespect.

We returned to our suite in silence, but the moment the door slid closed behind us, I locked it, using a personal security code reserved for the highest-ranking officers at the

IQC. Besides me, Rager and Liam, no one but one of the kings could override the locks.

Liam was facing me, Bella and Rager behind him, when I turned away from the door.

"Evon," he said, then sighed. "You shouldn't have done that."

"No. I should have done it a long time ago." When he opened his mouth to protest, I raised my hand in a gesture I knew probably looked almost exactly like my father had a few short minutes ago. "I will not yield nor change my mind."

That stopped him from speaking, his mouth parted as if he were about to argue, but I dismissed his rebuttal with a wave of my hand.

"This family is mine. Bella is ours. No one will break us. No one." Bella hadn't moved, her hand in Rager's, but her eyes widened as I took a step toward her. She had no idea what I'd just done, what Liam and I were talking about. "You were magnificent, Bella. So proud. So strong. A worthy mate."

Her cheeks darkened and I knew Rager squeezed her hand in agreement, but I was in a strange mood. The threat to my new family crystallized for me just how crucial protecting it was. And that powerful new understanding drove me now, to reassert my claim as the dominant in the room. This was my family, my mate. They were mine to protect, mine to pleasure, just...mine.

"Take off your clothes, Bella."

She shook her head to argue. "I need a work station or a computer. Something I can use to start learning your coding system. This NPU thing is amazing." She tapped her fingers to her temple. "It helped me decipher that tablet in record time, thank god, but I need more time if I'm going to crack open the military communications system."

Her mind was not where I wanted it to be.

"Take. Off. Your. Clothes."

"Evon. But what about—"

"After we fuck you, mate. After you scream. After you know who you belong to."

Her mouth fell open. "But I already do. I need a computer. I want to—"

"No." I was not used to one so defiant.

Rager chuckled and let go of her hand, stepping back to admire the delicious curves that would soon be on display. He had patience and saw amusement in the lack of mine.

"By the gods, Evon. Now?" I mentally scoffed at Liam's tone. As if he'd ever *not* want Bella. He shrugged, the rise and fall of his shoulders the barest hint of movement in my peripheral vision. His mind was in the wrong place as well. We'd figure out what the fuck was going on. Later. Now we had to reconnect as a family, and that was with Bella. Because of her.

She was what pulled us together, made us one.

"Fine." I saw the way Liam's cock began to swell beneath the pants he'd been given, knew he wasn't giving in to the charges against him. He just had to get his mind on what was important. "But they dragged me out of here, down the hall bare assed, my balls hanging out. I need to clean up."

He disappeared into the bathing room and I knew he'd return soon.

Or...not. An image of Bella naked and wet, covered in bathing oil and bubbles teased my mind with possibilities.

Hard nipples. Soft pussy. Round ass. Wet. All over.

With a growl, I rushed her and lifted her over my

shoulder to follow Liam into the bathing room. The shower was already on, the running water flowing over Liam's naked form.

Rager followed at a much more leisurely pace, his usual temperament back in full force at the pleasure he knew awaited. He was content to take it in any way I chose. He wasn't picky or demanding as I was.

Liam turned in the stall, his body covered with water, his cock already hard. At the door, Rager began to undress, pulling his uniform tunic up over his head as I set Bella down on her feet.

She looked up at me, her breathing fast, her eyes dark with desire. Yes, now she was in the right mindset. "Evon."

My name. Nothing more. No arguments or resistance. She didn't try to hide from me, instead meeting my gaze with acceptance. Surrender.

Submission.

With a groan, I lifted my hands to her cup her face and kissed her, exploring with a ravenous appetite to taste, to conquer. I learned her flavor with my tongue.

When she clung to me, boneless and weak—and just from a kiss—I lifted my head and grinned. "I warned you, mate."

A little V formed between her brows. "What?" The question sounded almost sleepy.

I lifted my hands to the neck of her cream tunic and ripped the offending fabric in half, exposing her heavy breasts, the delicate roll of her shoulders, the long, feminine line of her back. Her pants were next, forgotten scraps that landed in a heap on the floor. She stood naked but for a pair of soft boots lined with fur.

Her breathing was ragged, her hands at her sides. Yes,

she was the one for us. She didn't hide her body, but stood proud, stood powerful, knowing she affected us.

"Gods." Liam's gaze was transfixed on her round ass as he stroked his cock.

I shifted mine in my pants. If I stripped, this would be over too soon. She was *that* alluring, tempting, perfect. I might be the dominant one, but she had all the fucking power.

"You want that ass, brother?" I dropped to my knees before her and took her hands in mine, tugging her forward so that she was bent at the waist, her ass open and on display for Liam within the shower. "You can't have it. Not yet."

With a growl, Liam stepped out of the enclosure, sliding the screen aside and moved in behind her. His body was dripping with water, his cock hard and pointed straight at her, eager to fuck, pussy or ass. He pushed two fingers into her pussy. I watched Bella's face, the way her eyes widened at Liam's sudden intrusion, the way she gave over to it, reveled in what he was doing with just those digits.

"No, but I can have this," he growled. "Her pussy is so fucking sweet." Bella shook as he slowly moved his fingers in and out of her body, the wet, slippery sound of fucking making my cock jump as he grinned. Her breasts swayed with each shift of her hips. "She's wet. So hot for us."

Bella moaned and placed her hands on my biceps for balance, rested her cheek on my shoulder to gaze over at Rager as Liam continued to work her body like a master. Unable to resist, I used my hands to play with her breasts, the hard nipples hanging down toward the floor were a blatant invitation I could not deny.

Keeping one hand on her breast, I fisted the other in her

hair and shifted her slightly so that just the back of her head rested on my shoulder, so she couldn't help but look at Rager. "Fuck her mouth, Rager. You want his cock, don't you, mate?"

"She just got wetter. Damn, she's dripping."

I felt her try to nod as Liam confirmed her eagerness for our rough play. I released my hold and she turned her head to look in my eyes. She was close, so close, and I could see the gold flecks in her eyes. The lust. The need.

"Fill her up as Liam takes her pussy."

Rager was naked now, grabbed a towel and wet it, wrapping it around his hard cock to make sure our mate would find him pleasing to the taste. Reaching between my legs, I stuck my hand down my pants and rolled several drops of pre-cum off the head of my cock onto my fingertips.

"I don't need that to want you three."

I held my fingers up between us and we stared at the glistening fluid together.

"We won't go easy," I told her, ensuring she knew just how this time would be.

"I know," she replied, and the way she met us, need for need, had another drop of fluid seep from me.

Taking his place standing beside me, Rager held his cock at the ready, just beyond the reach of Bella's plump lips. All she had to do was turn her head.

"We take her together."

One hand twisting her nipple, I slid the other over her abdomen and down to her clit, brushing it with my pre-cum. She didn't need it. No. She was so fucking hot and ready for us. But we weren't going to be gentle. As her Dominant, it was my job to ensure her safety, her comfort, her happiness. Her pleasure. I would not deny her one bit of it.

Liam positioned himself behind her, slid his cock up and down her folds, eyeing me.

I nodded to both of them as Bella bit her lip, muffling her groan as the seed power enveloped her.

"Now."

9

I WAS LOST, COMPLETELY DRENCHED IN A WAVE OF DESIRE. I'D been so hot and eager for my mates even without the damn seed power. The way they'd stood up for each other in the courtroom—or whatever the hell it was called on Viken— made me proud to be their mate. It made me hot. They were so rugged, virile and potent I'd wanted to jump each one of them. But now, I wanted them to jump me. I was content to let Evon have his bossy way with me because, damn. I liked it. I liked turning off all my thoughts and just feeling.

I loved being wanted so badly they couldn't wait, couldn't stop themselves from taking me. This suite felt like my own personal kingdom and everything here was mine. They were mine. Totally, completely devoted. Obsessed.

And with the seed power? I couldn't do anything but melt under their attention. It was the most wicked drug and

I was addicted. There would be no relief, not with these three. And I wanted none.

My clit swelled and pulsed from Evon's fingers, from the potent seed he coated it with. I moaned, gripped his biceps. My inner walls clenched, eager to be filled. We'd fucked only a few hours earlier, but I wanted more. I never wanted this feeling to end, at least not until I had my men filling me up with their thick, hard cocks and pumping me full of their seed.

I wanted every thick spurt of it. I looked at Rager's cock, so close to my mouth, the pre-cum glistening on the tip and my mouth watered for the taste of it.

God, what was wrong with me? My thoughts were so dirty. I definitely had a strong sexual appetite, but I'd never craved the taste of a man's cum. I was surrounded and overpowered and I loved it. I wanted to give them anything they wanted. I needed to give them everything, make them lose control, break them.

I pushed back and worked my inner muscles to make sure my pussy tightened in invitation around Evon's fingers. "I want you, Liam. Do it."

"No." Liam's voice cut through the haze of my need.

Lifting my head, my gaze flipped up to see Evon glancing at my other mate. His eyes were so pale, so clear, his jaw strong. Proud. Kissable. I wanted his mouth. I wanted his tongue. I wanted to bury my fingers in his hair and devour him as Liam filled me from behind. God, it was so wrong, but I wanted to kiss one man and fuck another.

"I want your ass, mate." Liam's big hand slid down over my bottom, his thumb slipping in between to brush over the virgin entrance he seemed to want so badly.

"Yes," I groaned. I had no idea there was so much

feeling, so much…sizzle by being touched there. And he hadn't even done more than circled over the sensitive skin.

"No," Evon replied. "She's not ready. The seed power will dull any pain she might feel. We could hurt her."

Liam continued to press and circle his thumb, pushing a little harder now, coaxing my tight ring of muscle to open for him. "You think I'd just take her unprepared?"

I glanced at Evon, but Rager stole my attention. He walked over to a table and grabbed a small bottle. Ah, the lube from earlier. Glancing down at me, he winked, then tossed the lube to Liam. I assumed he caught it because I heard the lid opening, felt a cool stream of fluid drip over the seam of my bottom and Liam captured it with his thumb, worked it in more and more with additional pressure until all at once I flowered open.

I moaned at the hot stretch, the slight burn. "More," I said, flicking my gaze to Evon as I bit my lip. I felt Liam's thumb. It felt huge working the lube into me, huge and foreign and right. I imagined what it would feel like with a hard cock in both my pussy and my ass. Imagined the stretching, the slight pain, the feeling of being overwhelmed, taken, impaled and fucked.

Once they had me full, so full, I'd grab the third one and swallow him down. Rule all three of my mates at once. Own them like they owned me. I'd be so good, so hot and wet and tight. I'd wrap them up and make them buck and shout, lose their minds.

I'd be a goddess. A sex goddess and they'd worship me.

"She has three mates. She needs more than Liam's thumb." Rager's voice was laid back, but I heard the bite of command in it. "Move, you dominant bastard."

Evon's eyes widened, but he shifted so his hand on my

one shoulder held me up.

"Let's see how many times you can come riding my face before Liam has your ass all nice and stretched for his cock." Rager winked at me, then dropped down onto the floor on his back. He slid backward so his head was between my knees. Hooking his hands on my parted thighs, he tugged me down so I was sitting...oh fuck.

Right. On. His. Face.

"Oh fuck." This time I said the words aloud and I could feel Rager's smile on my pussy.

"With you licking her pussy, we'll be here all night," Evon protested.

Rager growled his assent and sucked my clit into his mouth, hard. I whimpered and gave up fighting. Lifting my ass in the air, I ground down on his face like a bad, bad girl. I wanted more. Rager's hands clenched on my thighs, pulling me down harder as his tongue dove deep, then out, licking me. Stroking my clit. Fucking me.

"Don't be such a baby," Liam said. He coaxed more and more lube up into me, his palm on my bottom as he worked his thumb inside my tight back opening. For being so big, he was really gentle, if that was the right adjective for being thumb fucked in the ass. He was good at this, knowing my body better than I did.

Rager did, too, because I was about to come.

"Get in her mouth," Liam said, being the bossy one. "Bella, you want to suck Evon's cock, don't you? I think your mate is feeling neglected. Swallow him down so he shuts up and lets us fuck you."

Evon grunted or some other manly growl sound in his chest as he shifted position, stepping over Rager's legs so that he stood in front of me, cock bobbing. He kept a big hand on my shoulder, taking some of my weight as my arms trembled. I put a hand on his muscled thigh, my other gripping the base of his cock. My fingers didn't even close around it.

Earlier, before we'd been interrupted, I'd been about to suck all three of my mates' cocks. I'd thought nothing could ease the seed power's hold on me, but several guards had done the trick, completely ruining the mood. Not this time.

Now, nothing was going to stop us from having each other. Nothing was going to stop me from taking Evon's big cock down my throat, sucking him until he couldn't hold back, until he shot his hot cum onto my tongue. I knew I was going to come the second it coated my mouth. I practically tugged him by his cock so I could get my mouth on him, to get my tongue to flick and swirl over his broad crown.

A sound escaped my throat. I wasn't sure if it was because Liam had switched his thumb for two of his fingers, stretching me farther, or if it was because Rager's tongue knew just how to flick my clit, or because I tasted a hot pulse of Evon's pre-cum.

"Is she ready?" Evon asked.

Liam's fingers were scissoring and sliding, fucking my ass as I knew his cock would soon. "Bella, mate." A loud crack filled the room a second before I felt the hot sting of his palm against my right ass cheek. "He's still talking."

The spanking surprised me, pushed me forward until Evon's cock bumped the back of my throat. I swallowed and he groaned.

"She just dripped all over my face," Rager said, his warm breath fanning over my pussy. "She likes a good, sound spanking. Do it again."

Liam spanked me again as he added another finger into my ass.

I wanted Evon mindless, completely swamped with pleasure, as I was. I shifted my hand so I cupped his balls, my fingers brushing over the smooth skin behind.

"By the gods," he growled and his hips bucked, pushing his cock into my throat again. I breathed through my nose as he began to gently fuck my mouth, pulling back so I could take a deep breath, then going deep again.

Just as they found all the places that made me hot, I discovered Evon liked his taint played with. And so I continued and I felt his balls draw up close to his body, his hips moving in an uneven rhythm. Rager flicked my clit just right and I came, moaning. The vibrations must have been too much for Evon because he groaned, swelled in my mouth and flooded it.

I swallowed, again and again, taking in his plentiful seed. At the feel of it on my tongue, I braced for the burn of his seed power flooding my system. Within seconds it hit me like a cannon blast of pure flame. I came again, the spasms as I wiggled on Liam's fingers, drawing out my orgasm into endless aftershocks as Rager suckled my clit. I couldn't think. I was an animal, my body taking control as my mates kept me on the edge.

I heard Evon's ragged breathing as I slowly came back to myself. Rager gently kissing my pussy as Liam's fingers continued their relentless preparation.

Evon exhaled a deep breath, pulled out of my mouth. He cupped my chin so I looked up at him, his thumb swiping a drop of his seed from the corner of my mouth and I licked it off.

I should have been done in. Two orgasms in rapid

succession, but I wasn't. I hadn't been fucked yet and I wanted them inside me, needed the connection. This was wonderful, powerful, but it wasn't enough. "Please."

No demand from me this time. I was begging, and I hid none of my need from Evon. His eyes were glazed with his own release, but I saw something else there, a tenderness I'd never seen from him before. "Do you want Liam to fill your ass, Bella?"

"I need..." Well, I wasn't sure what to say, how to put it into words. It wasn't about an orgasm. This was more. So much more.

"She's ready," Liam said.

Rager kissed my clit one last time, then slid out from between my legs. Evon moved to let him come up to his knees. "I don't want you fucking her ass while I'm down there. I don't want your balls slapping into the top of my head."

While he was serious, the tone of Rager's voice was playful and I heard Liam laugh as he slipped his fingers free.

"She deserves a bed if she's going to give you her virginity," Evon ordered.

Rager scooped me up and carried me into the other room and the big bed. Evon was there first, grabbing two pillows and placing them in a stack at the edge of the mattress. Putting me back on my feet, Rager leaned down and kissed me, then straightened, held my gaze. "Ready?"

I appreciated his concern, this check-in before I did something crazy, like taking Liam's big cock up my ass. I glanced to my right and saw Liam lubing up, coating his cock so that it glistened.

Yeah, it was worth an ask. I flicked my gaze back to Rager's amber eyes and lifted my hands to his bronze head. I pulled him down and kissed him again, begging him to fuck me with my mouth. He crushed me to his broad chest and took what he wanted, tongue going deep, tasting me as I tasted my pussy on his tongue. The mixture of flavors exotic and forbidden.

I was so very bad, I was sure my parents would be rolling over in their graves, and I didn't care. I tore my mouth from his and looked at Liam, who was watching us with one hand around his cock and his gaze glued to my parted lips. "Oh, I'm ready."

Liam came up, took my chin from Rager and kissed me just as Rager had, hard, demanding, as if he'd never get enough. When he pulled back, he rested a palm on my ass and stroked my empty hole, still well lubricated and ready for him. "That's right. You're ready and you're going to love it. Know how I'm sure?"

I shook my head.

"Because you're my perfect match."

Rager helped me lean forward over the pillow, even lifted me up so I was bent over the bed. With the added height of the two pillows under my hips, my feet didn't even touch the floor, the bed was so big. It was made for huge Vikens, not dainty Earth women who were going to get their ass fucked.

The pillows were soft, the room warm. My skin was sensitive, I had the taste of Evon's seed in my mouth, the seed power raging through my veins.

Rager sat down on the bed on my right, Evon on my left. They each took one side of my bottom in their hand and opened me for Liam, holding the soft mounds of my ass wide, pulling me open so the stretching sensation made me gasp even before Liam stepped close. If I wasn't so damn horny I would have been embarrassed. I knew all three of my mates had a full view of my eager pussy and prepared back entrance.

Fucking these three wasn't demure. It wasn't prudish. It was hot and carnal, wet and dirty. It was fucking.

And I wanted more. I wanted Liam to take what he wanted, to give me exactly what I needed. He was right. I would like what he was about to do because we were matched. I took a deep breath, let it out. Propped up on my elbows, I looked over my shoulder, saw Liam, cock in hand, watching me. Waiting.

"I want all three of you." I was beyond shame. I wanted a hard cock in my pussy. I wanted to suck Rager down as Evon fucked me and Liam filled me from behind. I wanted to *own* these men the way they owned me. Totally. Completely.

Evon smacked me on the ass, the sting making me squirm. "Soon, mate. But you've only been here one day. You have thirty days to accept the match. If we fill you together, the official claiming will be complete. There will be no recourse for you. No second chance."

"No changing your mind," Rager added.

Evon leaned over to whisper in my ear. "You make us crazed, Bella. But we will not take you in the heat of the moment. Not like this. Once we claim you, it's forever."

I licked my lips, then nodded. I understood. I could even appreciate their thoughtfulness. But I was still aching and empty. "Liam." His name on my lips was a demand. Nothing less.

He took the step that separated us, aligned his cock at my last virgin place and carefully pressed inward. I felt a finger sliding and circling around the head of his cock, pressing and stretching my skin to ease the way.

Hands slid up and down my sweaty back, soothing me. Rager leaned down so he was propped up on his own elbow and I could look into his face. He glanced down my back, watched Liam, his golden gaze darkening with heat.

"So fucking hot, Bella. Let him in. Open up and let him fuck you. I want to watch."

His tone wasn't commanding like Evon's would be. It held promise, reassurance that what Liam was doing would be something I loved. Rager wouldn't let anyone, even my other mates, touch me in any way that I didn't like. Knowing he was there watching out for me, with me, I relaxed my arms, dropped all the way onto the bed.

Evon's hand stroked over my hair, brushed it back from my face.

I sighed then and that was the moment Liam popped inside.

I tensed, but they were all talking to me. *Good girl. Yes, I'm inside. Look how you take Liam's cock. He's going so deep. You're so sexy, Bella. So hot. You like this? You want more?*

Coaxing and praise, dirty words and promises, Rager and Evon said it all as Liam began to fuck me in slow, deep strokes. In. Out. A hot glide of hard man conquering my last virgin hole, filling me up, marking me in a way I knew I'd never get over, never forget. This was forever. I'd be his forever, theirs forever, overwhelmed, fucked until I could barely walk, until my body was limp with exhaustion. Sated. They'd never tire of me, never want another, and the knowledge made me burn.

I whimpered and gasped, clawed the blanket and eyed Rager, then Evon. "More."

10

ella

"Like it, mate?" Liam asked, his voice rough with his need as he thrust forward a bit harder, shifting me on the bed until Rager and Evon both used a hand on my shoulder to steady me for Liam's thrusts.

My eyes rolled up into my head and my hands cramped where I fisted the blanket and tightened everything, clamping down on the huge cock filling me.

Liam groaned and I squeezed him harder. "Shit, when you grip me like that, I'm going to come."

I did it again.

"Fuck, you want me to come?"

He spanked my ass lightly. Knowing it was giving him pleasure had me doing it again and again. So, of course, I kept squeezing and he kept spanking me.

Evon reached beneath me, found my clit, used two

fingers to pinch and pull, then rub in a steadily increasing rhythm.

Rager leaned in and took my mouth, tongue thrusting deep in time to Liam's fucking. A broken cry left my throat as Liam placed both hands on my inner thighs and pushed me open, the cold air of the room hitting my exposed pussy as Evon moved, slipping two fingers in my wet core from under me as Liam pressed deep. Deeper.

"Come for us, mate," Evon commanded. "Strangle Liam's cock."

I couldn't take any more pleasure. It was like a dam in a rainstorm, filling and filling, then breaking over the banks.

I tensed, a scream lodged in my throat as every nerve ending in my body, every single one surrounding Evon's fingers and Liam's cock awoke, flared.

Rager caught my scream with his kiss, his hands a tight fist in my hair, holding me in place for the bucking motion of Liam's hips.

"Fuck, I can't hold back." Liam's words accompanied a hot pulse of seed filling me. He groaned, held himself still, his hips pressed against my stinging ass as his seed filled me, coating me on the inside.

Evon wiggled his fingers, finding the sensitive place inside me as my pussy reacted to Liam's seed, the orgasm going on and on until I couldn't breathe, thought my heart was going to explode from my body. When it was over, Evon's fingers stroked slowly in and out of me, more a caress than fucking now. Rager let go of my hair and soothed me, stroking my back as his kiss gentled into something sweet. Patient. Adoring.

I felt cherished. Protected. Safe. My body was so far gone that even Liam's seed power was only a slight stir in my blood now, a heat that made me want to stretch and turn onto my back, open my legs and let them fill my pussy over and over for hours.

God, I was never going to get enough of this. Of them. And I was positive that wasn't the seed power talking.

Liam and I were both breathing hard, our skin coated in sweat. Slowly, carefully, he pulled out and I felt his seed slip from me.

I felt myself being moved, rolled onto my back just as I'd imagined. But my eyes were closed and already I missed the exquisite pleasure mixed with the bite of pain. My ass was sore and my bottom tingled from being spanked, but it morphed into a hot glow.

I didn't open my eyes until I felt a cock sliding into my pussy. I was so wet, the penetration was easy. My eyes fluttered open and I met Rager's dark golden gaze. He smiled at me, used his hands to caress my breasts, his touch gentle. Reverent.

"My turn," he said. I smiled up at him and wrapped my hands around his wrists, holding him to me as I lifted my hips to take him deeper.

"Yes, Rager. Fill me up," I demanded. My pussy had been too empty when the last orgasm hit me. Empty. The tissue so swollen, so tight, that I groaned and bit back a cry with even the soft slide of his hips. He was taking his time, my mate. "Too slow," I protested, but he just laughed.

"I am a patient man."

"I'm not," Evon interrupted, shoving Rager's hands off my breasts so his mouth could take their place. He worked my nipples, sucking them as Rager fucked me. One of Evon's hands found its way down the bed to my ass and he pulled me open once more, taking my bare bottom in hand and pulling wide.

Rager sank deeper with a groan and lifted his hand to my opposite thigh, pushing me so that my pussy was spread open from both directions. "Gods, Evon. You're a bastard."

Rager's neck corded as his cock leapt and jumped, coating me with his seed.

Evon didn't even lift his head from my nipple, just smiled as he took it into his mouth. My back arched up off the bed and I buried my hands in Evon's hair as Rager's seed power hit me and a slow, rolling orgasm moving through me like melted caramel, slow and sticky and so damn delicious.

Evon lifted his head and grinned like a naughty little boy. "My turn."

Before I could react, he took Rager's place. His huge cock slid into me in one hard, fast stroke. Where Rager had been slow, languorous, Evon was the opposite, every thrust deliberately forceful, measured, demanding my body to respond. Both hands dropped to my abdomen and he used one set of fingers to stroke my clit as he moved, fucking me like a machine, driving me over the edge.

Pussy pulsing, I hooked my legs about his waist and locked my ankles behind him, holding him deep inside me as I exploded yet again.

When I caught my breath, my mate was staring down at me, devouring me with his eyes. "You're so fucking beautiful, mate. I'm going to make you come again."

On either side of the bed, the other two watched as he started to move once more, desire and contentment in their gazes. I wasn't sure if I was going to survive my mates, this pleasure, but as Evon kept his promise I thought this might be a good way to go.

————

BELLA, IQC CORE COMMAND CENTER

THE CURVED WORKSTATION CHAIR WAS PADDED, MADE FOR long hours without much movement. But I shifted regularly from side to side. My bottom was sore from too much... ummm...yeah. I wasn't going to think about that right now. A bag of frozen peas would have helped, but I wasn't going to ask for that, even if they knew what peas were.

Evon sat behind me as two IQC security officers monitored us, or rather, monitored me through the video system. I knew their cameras were pointed to watch every move of my fingers on their controls, every flicker and switch on the screen. I'd been at it for hours, my mind in that sacred place where things made sense without reason, where I saw patterns I shouldn't be able to see, where information flowed into my mind and was processed on a nearly subconscious level.

Programmers and hackers alike lived for this moment, the moment when we became one with the machine, one with the strange language used to command it. There was no real way to describe the feeling when everything clicked, the unthinkable made perfect sense, when I could communicate with the system in an intuitive way that I could never explain.

I'd always been good with code, from my early teens I'd been able to make computers do what I wanted even though there were times that even I didn't fully understand how I was able to do what I did.

Other times, my choices were deliberate and cruel,

meant to break someone else's design, crack their code open and make it bleed, strangle the system, force a program to self-destruct.

But now? God, with the NPU that Warden Egara had planted in my head? She'd told me the device was meant to integrate with the language center of my brain and act as a translator, helping me understand all the languages of the Coalition Fleet. Sure, I could understand my mates, even though some part of me knew they weren't speaking English. But the code in my mind? The extra brainpower I now had available to process language and patterns? It was like I *was* the machine. The control I'd had before, to command a system to do exactly what I wanted it to do, was tenfold. Maybe more.

"Holy shit. I'm a fucking A.I.," I breathed.

"What, mate? Is there a problem?" Evon rose at once to loom behind me like a shadow. I felt his breath fan my neck, his hands resting on my shoulders.

I shook my head and waved him off with a negligent flick of my wrist, barely acknowledging his question, although the heat of his hands lingered even after he sat back down. I didn't want to talk to him. I didn't want him here, not right now. I needed to be in my bubble where the code flowed through me like my birth language and nothing else existed. I was in *The Zone,* and I didn't want him or anyone else to take me out of it. If they distracted me now, it could take me hours to get back to this point.

And I was about to break their system wide open. For Liam. For all of us.

Just...one...more...

"Got it." Satisfaction and triumph poured through me and I was in. Just like that, their entire system was laid bare.

I saw the network of commands, the firewalls around the individual security codes, the system in place to protect them.

And I dismantled it all in moments and went looking for what I knew must be there.

Someone had accessed Liam's codes, and that kind of thing always left a trail of breadcrumbs for me to follow. A few minutes later, I had it. A workstation ID. A time stamp.

Shortly after that? The security camera feed. An empty chair. Someone approaching. Blonde hair. A face I recognized. My eyes widened as I stared at the display.

"Oh, shit," I whispered.

"What is it, mate?" Evon stood directly behind me once again, looking over me as I watched a recorded security feed in the bottom corner of the screen, as his sister sat down at a monitor and set Liam up to be charged for murder.

Evon's hand came to rest on my shoulder and he leaned in close to my ear, his voice the barest whisper of sound. "Is that Thalia?"

"Yes." I wasn't sure what to say. How do you tell a man you barely know that his own flesh and blood betrayed him? Betrayed everything he'd spent every day of his life trying to protect. Hell, she'd betrayed their entire family. I knew how Evon's brother and father felt about service to Viken.

"Turn it off. Now." The hand on my shoulder squeezed to the point of pain, but Evon abruptly let me go.

"But, what about the judicial panel? And Liam? We have to tell someone—"

He grunted. "No. Turn it off. There must be some mistake."

No way. I looked up at him, blinked, confused. "No. I'm sorry. It's not a mistake."

He backed toward the door. "Turn it off. Now. That's an order."

I rose to my feet, spun to face him. "I'm not a soldier, Evon."

"Turn. It. Off. Now!" He gently moved me aside and closed down the system, closing the window on hours of work in the span of a few seconds. His fingers slid over the controls with deft movements, proving he was more skilled at cyber work than he let on.

I slid back to block him. "What the hell are you doing?"

Those ice-blue eyes met mine. The usual heat I saw in them was missing now. "Leave this to me."

He was fucking kidding with this, right? "It took me hours to get that data, Evon. Hours." I waved my hands in the air as if that would help him get my level of frustration.

"I am aware of that, Bella. It's time to go." He tugged on my hand, trying to pull me toward the door, but I dug in my heels and refused to budge.

I was no match for his size and strength, but I was putting up a good resistance. "No. What about Liam? The hearing with your father is in less than three hours."

"Don't argue. It's time for you to go back to our quarters. I'll take care of it." His face had hardened even further, the pale blue of his eyes cold and unyielding, nothing like the heated blue flame I'd seen earlier when he was balls deep in my pussy, acting like I mattered. Like he cared. Like I meant more to him than his stupid family honor.

Does. Not. Compute.

I couldn't wrap my head around what was happening right now. Was Evon willing to betray Liam and Rager over this? To deny what Thalia had done? Just how far was he going to go to protect his *real* family, his sister? "Evon—I don't think you understand."

He ignored me and reached for the comm station in the wall. Pressed it with more energy than necessary. "Rager? It's Evon. Where are you?"

I heard my other mate's reply through the speaker. "Just returned from patrol."

Evon's chin went up. "Are you in our quarters?"

"Yes."

"Good." Evon eyed me as he spoke. "Don't go anywhere." He disconnected, or ended the transmission—whatever the hell it was called in space—and walked toward me. "Let's go, Bella. You've done your job. You've done enough."

I shook my head. "No."

"Now." He sighed. "I don't have time for you to throw a tantrum."

I was going to strangle him with my bare hands. I'd have to leap up in the air to pull it off, but I'd do it. I would.

Everything I thought I knew, the trust I'd handed over so easily was like the bitter taste of burned ash in my mouth. So much for honor on this damn planet. He'd rather hide the truth than harm his dear family. In return? *Our* family—Rager, Liam, Evon and me—never had a chance. The Tyrell family was no better than the corrupt political systems on Earth, the powerful protecting their own. Lies. Deceit. Exploitation. And I'd fallen for Evon, hard.

I'd fallen for the hope of something...more.

Biting back tears, I bit my lip to keep from saying something I knew I couldn't take back. If he wouldn't listen to reason, perhaps Rager or Liam would. Evon loved his sister, so I could understand how he'd try to rationalize this.

Why he'd want to assume I was wrong. Even with the clear proof he'd seen with his own eyes.

He opened the door and held out his hand to indicate I should precede him down the hall. I knew the way. The base wasn't large, and I'd always been exceptionally good at mental maps. When his hand landed on the small of my back, I pushed him away and stiffened my spine. His touch felt dirty now.

The five-minute stroll seemed to last an hour and when the door to our suite opened, only then did I dare glance back over my shoulder to find Evon's eyes burning with rage. Yeah, I wasn't too happy with him either.

"Go inside, Bella." His voice had a sharp bite to it. One I'd heard before when he was arguing with his brother, but never with me. "Rager will see to you."

With that, he turned on his heel and walked away, head held high, his jaw tense with stubborn pride and anger.

I crossed the threshold to our quarters, took in the rumpled bedding from our recent bout of wild fucking and realized that I'd made the classic female mistake, thinking that getting naked meant more than it did. That orgasms could fix everything.

Fucking. Yes. That was the right word. Evon had fucked me. Used me. And when push came to shove, he'd chosen his blood family, and his sister, over his mate.

I swallowed, trying to get rid of the painful lump in my throat. If the tears started, they wouldn't stop. I couldn't explain this to Rager if I was babbling like an idiot. I had to keep my shit together, talk in cold, hard facts. Data. That was what I had.

The entry door slid closed behind me and I heard Rager's voice from the bathing chamber. I walked closer, my intention to close the door so I wouldn't have to listen to him in the shower, imagine him naked. I wasn't in the right mindset for that kind of thinking.

Even furious, the thought of Rager filling me, soothing me with his patient brand of loving, was too great a temptation. I refused to be that weak. I refused to run to him and bury myself in pleasure just because Evon had broken part of my heart. I wouldn't be the needy, dependent female I so despised.

Now was not the time to give myself to him again. It would feel good, would make me forget for a little bit, but that was all. Everything ugly would still be there waiting once the orgasm faded.

No, I formulated my plan as I closed the distance. Rager would get out of the shower and dress. Then we'd call Liam and I would tell them both what happened. Sure, Evon wanted to protect his sister, but Liam was innocent, and I could prove it. Even with Evon's true loyalties elsewhere, I couldn't imagine he wanted his friend to be executed. I didn't know the laws or customs on Viken, but my mates did. And they knew Evon. We'd figure this out together.

Or was I wrong about that, too? I'd never been one of those people who intuitively knew what others were thinking. The opposite, in fact. I had trouble relating to people, found them, on the whole, difficult to talk to and lacking in common sense. I'd been told I was odd, quirky and distracted, difficult to talk to, hard to read.

Maybe it was me. Maybe my lack of spectacular people skills was going to really hurt this time. Maybe I just didn't know enough about the men I was mated to, or about their history. Could I be so wrong about my mates? Was the Interstellar Brides Processing system not as fantastic as they claimed? Could three men hold me down and fuck me like I was their whole world when actually I meant nothing to them?

Yes. Yes, they could. I didn't want to think it, didn't even want to consider the possibility, but on the whole, I was a realist. This whole Bride thing had been a wild hope, throwing my cards to the wind and hoping for a winning hand.

I wiped one stray tear from my eye and shook myself from head to ankle, breaking the stranglehold of my thoughts. No. Whatever the answers were, Liam was innocent and I could prove it. He wasn't going to die, not when I could save him. And now that I'd been inside the Viken security networks, getting back to where I'd been wouldn't take me long.

Lifting my hand to the bathroom door's manual control, I was about to wave my palm over the panel when I heard a distinctly feminine voice within.

"Give me that big cock, Rager. Don't make me beg."

11

"Give me that big cock, Rager. Don't make me beg."

Shock held me frozen in place. Clenching my teeth, I swallowed hard. That voice. I knew that grating, feminine voice. I didn't want to see what was going on in that room, but I couldn't risk being wrong. Not about this.

Peeking around the edge of the doorframe, I leaned in just enough to catch sight of a naked feminine body walking toward the shower. Rager was out of view, but the woman swaying her hips as she approached the shower was tall and lithe, strong, with long blonde hair hanging free halfway down her back. She held her breasts cupped in her hands like offerings as she licked her lips with an eager smile on her face, waiting for my mate's *big cock.*

Thalia.

I hadn't known her long, but I didn't know many people

on Viken. My three mates, Dravon, Evon's father, Thalia. I'd spent time with Thalia and I'd trusted her because I trusted Evon. She'd even helped me pick out clothes like a BFF.

Big mistake. I knew someone on Viken had stolen her heart. I wasn't a social butterfly, but I had managed to catch on to that fact in the short time I'd spent with her. She'd been nice to me, but now? Thalia was fucking Rager?

No. Rager was fucking Thalia.

So who was the woman on the side? Her? Or me?

Pulling back silently, I left them to it and ran on tip-toes to the door. Thankfully, Viken doors slid open and closed silently and Rager—and his fuck buddy—hadn't known I'd even been there. I had no idea where I was going, just...away.

Stumbling down the hall in a daze, I shivered and wrapped my arms around my stomach as nausea rose to choke me. God, I was such an idiot. I'd fallen in love with these men, totally bought into the lie of the *perfect match,* the one true mate who would fulfill all of my subconscious desires. A mate, or mates, who would want me as I was. Accept me for who I was.

Love me.

They were supposed to love me. Put me first. Take care of me forever. We were supposed to be a team, a family, an unbreakable unit with an unbreakable bond.

We were matched, for fuck's sake.

The strangled laughter that erupted from my body held no hint of humor. Pain roared through me like a lion camped out in my brain, rattling my bones from the inside until it felt like even my eyes trembled. I couldn't think. Couldn't focus. All I could do was feel, and the self-hatred was getting pretty heavy, weighing me down until I rounded my back and hunched my shoulders like an eighty-year-old woman.

Stupid. I was a freaking genius, right? Could hack almost any system, write complex code in my sleep, and I'd fallen for the oldest trick in the book. They'd used me, used my body, made me believe they cared about me.

I'd fallen in love with them, and that was the worst pain of all. I'd given them everything, heart and body and soul. And the whole time they'd been lying.

Evon chose his family over the truth, and ultimately over me. He'd acknowledged my abilities, but turned his back on them. He'd turned his back on me. I couldn't live with a mate who denied the truth. Hid it to protect others. It was the very reason I'd traveled all the way across the damn universe, to avoid just this scenario. But no. Stupid shit and petty people were everywhere.

And that included Rager. I ran my hand over my face, tugged on my hair as I walked. Two warriors moved out of my way as I passed. God, Rager!

He was the sweetest one, the gentle one. At least with me. I never knew anyone so patient. If I hadn't come so quickly, I had no doubt he would have kept his head between my thighs for hours to get me off. He had a quick smile and a hard cock. I'd thought they were both just for me, for his fucking matched mate, but no.

How long had this thing with Thalia been going on? I wasn't a virgin, and while they hadn't said it outright, there was no way Evon, Rager or Liam were virgins either. They'd fucked before and obviously Rager had fucked Thalia. Was *still* fucking her.

It had been a day. A damn day and he couldn't keep his

hands off her. They'd taken me twice in twenty-four hours, and that wasn't enough for him?

"Such bullshit." Enough. Two out of three of my mates were assholes.

Wait. I stopped in my tracks, a huge lightbulb going off. Evon was protecting Thalia. Rager was fucking Thalia. Did that mean they were in on the scheme to frame Liam? Were they *helping* Thalia? Were they both working with her? Were they transporting stolen goods? I hadn't seen the footage where the poor guard they'd mentioned was murdered, but had Rager or Evon been the ones to do it? Oh god. Was I mated to murderers?

What about Liam? He was being framed for all this, and if the truth didn't come out, he was going to be executed. But Evon had made me turn off the monitors, walked away from the truth. When it was before him in full color, he turned his back.

But what about my other mate? Liam was innocent, being set up by his two closest friends. Close enough that they decided to share a mate. So far, Liam was perfect. Perfect for me.

Shaking my head, I ran my fingers along the smooth wall as I walked. I'd thought the other two perfect as well, but look where that got me. Wandering the damn halls.

No. I wasn't going to wander any longer. I didn't need to. I didn't *need* these mates. I had thirty days. Or twenty-nine, now. Whatever. By Interstellar Brides rules, I could refuse the mates they'd matched me to and I'd be matched to someone new.

It took me less than a day to be matched and transported halfway across the galaxy. I could be somewhere else on Viken before dinner.

Good. I stood still, looked around, trying to remember the layout of this station on the maps I'd seen earlier. My mind settled and the image of the grids of rooms and hallways, sections and stations appeared like magic.

At least my brain was still working. My heart hurt, had trusted this alien mating system, had thrown years of caution to the wind and *believed*.

No more. I figured out where the testing center was in relation to where I wandered and tried to keep my pace steady and measured as I made my way there.

The door slid open and a Viken man wearing the same burgundy and dark gray I'd seen on Warden Egara looked up from where he sat at his desk. He was older, perhaps sixty. The Interstellar Brides Program logo was on his chest and his eyes were kind. He reminded me of an old country doctor, the kind that held his patient's hands and gave lollipops to toddlers. He had a mild demeanor and a kind smile. I had to imagine he was good at making nervous warriors comfortable.

"I'm Warden Vora. You are the mate from Earth, arrived yesterday. Isabella Martinez." He stood up and bowed at the waist as he greeted me. "How may I assist you?"

The Viken was of similar size to my mates—no, they weren't my mates anymore. Looking around, I spotted the testing chair, identical to the one I'd sat in on Earth.

"I am here to exert my rights as a new bride. It hasn't been thirty days yet and I'd like new mates."

His graying eyebrows went up at my request.

"New mates? But, you already have three."

I nodded once. "Yes, I'm well aware of the number of men I was matched to. Trust me. But they aren't a good fit for me. Your system made a mistake. I need new ones," I repeated, not backing down one bit. I'd read the damn brochure, signed the stacks of paper. I knew my rights. I was supposed to give my mates thirty days to woo me, but they'd managed to blow this in one. Twenty-nine more was unacceptable.

The man began to wring his hands. "You are the first mate at the IQC that has encountered this problem."

I took a step farther into the room so the door slid closed behind me. "It's not a *problem*. It's a rule. If I do not wish to keep my mates within the first thirty days, I can request a new match."

God, was I going to get *three* new mates? Did I want less? Would I be satisfied with the attentions of a single man now that I'd had three?

The answer, I knew, was no. In less than a day, my new mates had ruined me. But there had to be other Viken trios looking for a bride. Vikens who weren't saboteurs, liars and murderers. Men who didn't cheat on their mates in the shower with tall blonde women with big tits and long legs— long, long legs. Much longer than mine.

"Have you been officially claimed? I can't arrange new mates if you belong to others."

I felt my cheeks heat, remembering all the things I'd done with my men. It had been dark and dirty, carnal and hot. Wild. But it also had been more. I'd felt a connection and I wasn't thinking of the stupid seed power or even love. No, it was a bond that went deep. I'd thought the match perfect. But no. All I'd been was used. I'd begged them to take me together, to claim me, and they'd told me no. It was too soon. They'd played it like they were protecting me from a rushed decision, from a lifelong commitment made in the heat of the moment. And here I stood, grateful that they hadn't given me what I wanted.

I was a fool.

And that was what made tears fill my eyes. At first I'd thought Evon had chosen family over me, that he was so loyal, so proud of his family's reputation and prestige that he was willing to lie to protect them. But no. It was more than that. He was complicit. He was one of them. And Rager? He wasn't simply *protecting* Evon's sister, he was *fucking* her.

A fresh batch of tears welled, spilled over. I swiped them away with my fingers.

"No. I haven't been claimed." I hopped up into the testing chair and spun so that my legs were settled as I relaxed back into the seat. If he wore a white jacket instead of a warden's uniform, I'd think I was at the dentist. "Let's get on with it." I swallowed hard, tried not to sniff. "I need new mates. I have to go to a hearing in a few hours in front of the commander. Once that's done, I'll be free to leave." I turned to look at him and caught his eye, making sure he saw just how serious I was. "And I'd like to leave immediately."

"Evon, Liam and Rager are good warriors. Good Vikens."

I laughed, but without an ounce of humor. "Liam is. The others…" I let the rest hang as I shrugged. I couldn't blame the warden for his cluelessness. I had been right there with him. Worse, because I'd given them my body, and my heart.

I dropped my head and covered my face with my hands as sobs racked my shoulders. Hot tears seared my palms. Yes, I was hysterical. Weak. Broken. Everything I detested. But I was allowed to have this damn pity party. I'd chosen space assholes over prison only to be fucked in the pussy and ass, then fucked again by their lies.

I heard the warden moving, speaking quietly, but I didn't look up. It didn't matter. Nothing mattered besides getting off this stupid fucking station and starting over. Again.

———

LIAM

"WHAT?" I SHOUTED, EVEN THOUGH THE WARDEN DIDN'T need me to be so loud to be heard through my wrist communicator, especially in the dining hall.

The group of guards around me looked up from their plates, some even paused while eating, instantly on high alert. I listened to the warden in the testing center repeat himself.

"Your mate is requesting to be reassigned. She's here, in the testing center. She's extremely upset. I think you'd better get down here."

I stood, my chair sliding over the floor before tipping over with a loud clatter.

My patrol team also stood, the three men ready to do whatever I commanded.

All conversation ceased in the room, turning to see the commotion, but I didn't give a damn about any of them. Bella was asking to leave me, leave us.

And she could do it. We hadn't claimed her. She'd asked, begged us to take her, and we'd refused. We'd left ourselves open to this and suddenly I didn't care if it was right or wrong. I just wished we'd taken her together, locked her to us for all time. Losing her to another now would crush us. She'd be the end of us.

"I'll be right there." I stalked out of the room and down the hall, ignoring my lunch, the chair and everyone's stares. When my team started to follow, I waved them off and they returned to their meal.

Bella wanted to be reassigned? Now? What the hell had happened since I left her? The last time I saw her she was in bed nestled between Rager and Evon, naked and sated from so many orgasms I'd lost count.

Now—just a few hours later—she wanted to leave us completely? Reject our match and be assigned to new mates?

I picked up my pace. Ran. People stepped out of my way, perhaps more from the look on my face than my pace. There was no fucking way she was getting reassigned. Something had happened with Rager or Evon. Or maybe both, but not with me. No, Bella was mine.

I wasn't letting her go.

When I entered the small room, she was sitting in the testing chair, head down, crying. I was breathing hard, my heart rate out of control. I was more panicked now than I'd ever been in any Hive battle. Bella was upset. Really upset. I had no idea what to do with a crying female, but this one was mine. I had to figure it out.

The warden looked equal parts worried and relieved. Without a word, he slipped from the room, the door sliding closed behind him. We were alone.

She looked so small, so vulnerable, I ached for her. Whatever it was, whoever made her hurt like this, I'd kill the man. Or at least maim him. Make him suffer as she suffered now.

I walked over to her, scooped her up in my arms. Only then did she gasp, realize I was here. I sat down on the testing chair—the exact spot where I'd been matched to her —with her settled on my lap. I rested my chin on top of her silky black hair, tucked her against my chest.

"Cry, let it out, and then you'll tell me what's happened." I kept my voice low and even, hoping to soothe her with more than my hold.

I felt her shake her head and try to pull out of my arms. "Liam. You don't understand. It's...it's bad."

"Bad enough to want to be reassigned?" I asked, staring at the far wall. Anger boiled up, but I tamped it down. "So bad that you want to leave me, Bella? Why?"

"I won't be mated to liars. To murderers."

I stilled then. I didn't breathe and I swear my heart skipped a beat. For this, I had to look at her so I slid her out of my hold and onto the testing chair beside me, pushed her back so she was reclined. I turned my upper body and put my hands on the chair's arms to pin her in place. Looking down at her, I saw the unshed tears in her dark, wild eyes.

"Explain."

She licked her lips, took a deep breath. "Evon and Rager. They're in on it."

"In on what?"

"On the thefts. Using your security code. The murder."

That, I was not expecting. Maybe Evon had been too dominant and scared her. That seemed unlikely given her eagerness to submit, but it was in the realm of possibility. I'd worried that perhaps she'd been denied an orgasm. Perhaps our seed power was too much for her small human body to process and she'd become overly emotional. I'd feared that perhaps she was homesick since Viken was most likely nothing like Earth.

But in a million years, I never expected her to say Evon

and Rager had gone bad. I didn't believe it, but Bella did, and that was what mattered.

"How do you know this?"

She narrowed her eyes at me, remained quiet.

"You don't believe me," she said finally, her voice cold. She tried to get past me, but there was no way I was letting her out of this chair. With one hand still on the armrest, I used the other to push her back, placing my palm between her breasts and holding her in place. Gently, but I would not relent.

"I believe you are convinced your words are the truth." Tears slid from her eyes again. I kept her gaze, ensured she was looking at me as I spoke. "But your words are serious and I wish to know what proof you have seen. You are intelligent. You have honor, mate, and wouldn't make false claims without reason."

She relaxed then. I kept my hand on her, not to hold her in place, but to feel the beating of her heart.

"Evon took me down to one of the command stations. It took me a few hours, but I hacked your security system."

I smiled. I couldn't help it. My beautiful, brilliant mate.

"I found out it was Thalia who used your security codes. Evon and I watched her do it. He saw the video. He got angry and ordered me to turn it off."

"Video?"

"The security footage, the moving images. I told him it wasn't you." She sobbed again as she continued. "It wasn't you, it was Thalia."

My eyes widened and I sat up. My mind began to spin with possibilities. More questions. My mate had broken into Viken's security system? Pride filled me at my mate's cleverness even as an unfamiliar ache squeezed my chest for the man I called friend, for our fragile new family.

Evon would be devastated. His sister had betrayed us all, betrayed her family? She was responsible for the security breach? The illegal transports? The death of the guard? Why? I lifted my hand to Bella's face and cupped her cheek. "I'm so proud of you, mate. But I don't understand. You said Evon and Rager are in on it? And Thalia? Fuck. Thalia?" I was about to add more, more about how broken Evon would be at this betrayal, but Bella yanked her face from my touch and turned away from me.

"No. That was Rager's job."

I frowned. "What?"

"Fucking Thalia." She tipped up her chin, her tears now gone. In their place was steely resolve, a woman scorned. Pain. Soul-shattering pain that would harden her heart against us forever.

"Explain."

"Rager is fucking Thalia."

I stood then, paced the small room, ran a hand over my long hair. I wanted to blurt out it was impossible, that Rager wouldn't do something like that. He thought of Evon's sister as his *own* sister. He wasn't interested in her. If he had been, he would have mated her years ago, the first time she asked him. She'd been after him for years. Her obsession with Rager was well known to everyone at IQC. But Bella was new here, didn't know the history.

How could Bella not feel Rager's devotion as her matched mate? Hell, his head had been between her thighs earlier in the day as I worked her ass. How could she question him? A few hours ago, I'd seen something in her eyes that made my entire body sigh with contentment.

Love. Trust. Tenderness. Things I'd not had from a woman before. From *my* woman. Rager and Evon were as entranced as I. I had served with them for years, knew them almost as well as I knew myself. They were devoted to Bella, as I was.

"Bella, there must be some mistake. You are our mate. We would die for you. Kill to protect you. Anything for you, mate. What you are saying is truly impossible." I glanced at her, looking for doubt in her gaze, for weakness. There was none. Instead I saw pain, the same pain that had begun to twist through my gut at the thought that she might leave me.

"Rager is fucking Thalia." She said it slowly this time, deliberately pronouncing every word. It wasn't a question. She had proof.

"You saw them together?" There was no other explanation.

"After Evon dumped me at our quarters, I went into our suite. Rager was in the shower so I walked over to close the door so I could think and..."

"And?" I didn't want to hear this, I really didn't, but I would be strong for her.

"I heard Rager and Thalia in the bathroom. Together. So I peeked around the door—" her voice faltered and she wrapped her hands around her stomach as if she were in horrible pain. She bent forward, rocking slightly back and forth like a hurt child.

"You saw them." I was trying to keep up. Rager and Thalia together in the shower? Evon growing angry with her for her discovery? Leaving her abruptly without explanation? None of this made sense to me, but Bella's pain was real. The look in her eyes was undeniable. She was not a fool, nor prone to hysterics, as she'd proven in the hearing yesterday. She'd faced off with Evon's father and held her ground. I had no choice but to believe what she said.

But nothing made sense. Evon had no love for his family, the tension between them had grown for years and came to a peak when Evon chose his new mate, his new family over the old. If Rager hadn't punched Dravon at the hearing, Evon would have. And Thalia? A traitor? A killer? No.

Rager and Thalia together?

"She was naked, Liam. Rager was in the shower already, and she was naked." Bella closed her eyes, a fresh tear sliding down her cheek. "And I *heard* her." Disgust was so thick on the words it was like acid to my ears.

"You heard them together?"

She nodded. "Thalia said, and I quote, '*Give me that big cock, Rager. Don't make me beg.*'"

It made no sense. None at all. I was trying to get my mind around all of this as she continued. I dropped back to the chair beside her.

"Evon's choosing Thalia over me. He forced me to turn off the displays, to shut down my access to the back end. He didn't want me looking any more into it. He blew me off and told me not to worry about it, to let him handle things, before dropping me off at our suite like I was so much garbage, a terrible inconvenience. And you should have seen his eyes, Liam." She took a breath, then another, glanced up at me through her damp lashes. "Evon was so angry. I thought he was mad at me, that he was angry at Thalia for getting caught. Maybe he was trying to figure out how to protect her. But then I heard Thalia with Rager, and I figured it out. Everything clicked, you know?

"They're all working together. Evon and Thalia and Rager. They're all in on it together." Bella lifted her small hand and cupped my face, the expression on hers no longer full of rage or anger or even hurt. No, all I saw was pity, and it was directed at me.

"They're working together. They framed you for murder, and the rest. I had to warn you, Liam. I had to warn you and I'll tell the commander the truth. I can't let them execute you. But after that, I can't stay. I just can't."

Pulling her close, I held her for long minutes as she sobbed into my chest, her pain soaking every cell in my body with dread. I ran my hand up and down her back, and when she calmed, I pulled away and took her face in my hands.

"I'm going to find out what's going on, Bella. I promise you." I kissed her softly, hoping it wouldn't be the last time I tasted her sweetness. No. It wouldn't be.

Decision made, I pulled away and held her gaze. "Stay here until the hearing. I'll let Warden Vora know that you're not to be disturbed. I'm going to find out what's going on. And if what you say is correct, I'll take you away from here myself, Bella. But you're mine, and I'm not giving you up."

12

L IAM WAS GONE. E VON WAS GONE. R AGER WAS…WELL, probably still balls deep in that bitch, Thalia.

All the pain I'd felt had hardened inside me into steel. Liam, sweet Liam, still wanted to believe in his friends. I hoped he was right. But I was a realist, right? And there was no arguing with cold, hard evidence.

Evon was prepared to lie and hide the truth to protect his sister, perhaps even to the point of seeing Liam falsely executed.

Rager had never truly been part of our family. He'd never been mine. All I could do now was wonder if he'd been thinking about *her* every time he'd been touching me.

That thought made me shudder.

And Liam. Well, I'd help him clear his name. Perhaps something could be salvaged from this? Perhaps not.

Would he be able to let go of his past? If I refused him, I'd be taking everything from him at once, his most trusted friends and me. His entire world would shatter and I'd be at the epicenter of the explosion.

I groaned, my head aching. I'd been trying to keep track of the time, but I knew time twisted in moments like this. Minutes seemed like hours, an hour like an eternity. I'd spent time in prison. I knew.

Pacing, I had my back to the door when I heard the soft whisper of it opening. I turned, expecting to see Warden Vora, who'd returned to check on me, bring me food and drink and try to keep me company. But I hadn't been much for small talk. After a few minutes of my monosyllabic responses followed by strained silence, he'd given up and left me alone.

"Yes, Warden. I'm fine. Thank you." The words were out of my mouth before I turned to smile politely and shoo him away.

"I'm not the warden, Bella." Thalia stood in the entryway. Behind her, I saw the limp form of Warden Vora. I gasped.

"Did you kill him, too?" I asked.

She raised a brow, and her space gun at the same time. "He'll be fine. I set the ion blaster to stun. I don't kill innocents."

I scoffed at that. "What about the guard that ended up dead?"

Thalia walked into the room and helped herself to a swig of the lightly sweetened juice I hadn't finished. She chewed slowly on several pieces of fruit and cheese as I watched. Waited. She wanted me to know we were on her time. Her schedule. She was in charge here. The whole while she barely blinked, and never took her eyes off me. "He was one of ours, turned informant. He was going to turn me in, so my friends took care of it."

"You have shit friends."

"No. I have true friends. Loyal friends. Friends who would die for me, kill for me." Her gaze grew heated and I finally noticed the disheveled state of her uniform, as if she'd put it on in a hurry and never quite straightened herself out. Her hair wasn't braided as I'd seen it every other time she'd been in uniform. It hung loose and tangled around her face, as if she'd been running her hands through it.

Or Rager had, as she'd given him a blow job and swallowed his seed power down like the lying bitch I knew she was.

"What do you want, Thalia?" I crossed my arms over my chest, cocked a hip. She might think she had the upper hand, but she'd fucked my mate and I was pissed. "You won already. *You won.* Why are you even here?" I had to ask. She had Rager. Evon was on her side, protecting her. The only thing standing between them and their goal— was me. Oh.

"You came here to kill me."

It wasn't a question, and she didn't deny it.

"Not exactly. But I do need to get rid of you. I can't have you around turning Rager's head." She moved toward me and swung her gun to the side. "Let's go, Bella. Out the door, take a left in the hallway. If you do anything stupid, I'll kill you, and then I'll kill Liam just because you made me angry."

I'd seen this scenario in a dozen movies, seen hostage situations on the news. In the past, I liked to think I would have been brave, stare down the barrel of the gun and tell the kidnapper or attacker to go fuck himself. Or herself.

But the moment she threatened Liam, I was hers and she knew it. Rager? She'd never hurt her lover. I wouldn't have believed the threat. Same with Evon. He was her brother, family.

But Liam? They'd already proven they were willing to sacrifice him, and I couldn't bear the thought.

I went where she told me to, my head held high. I was wearing the same style of cream-colored clothing and boots I'd worn before. They were fur lined and warm enough to keep the chill of the station away from me, but with Thalia at my back, I shivered anyway. What could I do? That wasn't just a gun, it was a space gun. She said she'd stunned the warden. It had settings, not just a bullet. And I'd shown up on Viken and gotten in the way of her having Rager. Or I was diverting his attention, at a minimum. The thought of sharing Rager with her made me nauseated. I had to assume she felt the same way, especially since we were actually mated. What I shared with him legally trumped whatever passion they had. That meant she was deadly.

I had to think of something. Wait for my chance and wrestle the weapon away from her.

God, I didn't want to kill her, but what if it was kill or be killed? Perhaps it was still set to stun?

I was running out of time and I knew it. But when we reached the final door at the end of the hall, my mind drew a blank. Nothing on the maps I'd seen came to mind.

"Open the door, Bella." She jabbed me in the back this time for good measure and I tried to hold in the gasp of pain as I did what she asked.

The door slid wide and I realized why I had no idea what was on the other side.

Nothing. Nothing but outside. Bitter cold. White.

"Go. Keep walking or die right here."

Blinking against the blinding reflection of light on snow, I took my first tentative step onto the planet itself and tried not notice as my tears instantly turned to ice on my cheeks.

———

Evon, IQC VIP Guest Quarters

"You made yourself clear earlier, Captain."

My father's voice was its usual bland tone, but with it came an indifference I'd not seen before. We were in the large guest quarters. While I stood just inside the doorway, he sat in a comfortable chair positioned for the best view out of the large window onto the frozen vista. I doubted he noticed the stark beauty laid out before him. The way the wind lifted whispers of snow into the sky, creating endless tiny rainbows of color. The way the snow glistened like an infinite sea of small stars on a white canvas. The sky was crystalline blue and so clear I could actually see other planets winking and sparkling in the heavens during the middle of the day.

I could name them all, had loved everything about outer space since I was a boy in school.

This place fit. I was content serving the Royal Guard here. The dangerous splendor of the icy tundra appealed to something inside me I'd never bothered to analyze and didn't care to explain. The air itself tasted wild, like risk and freedom locked in a never-ending dance.

My father? He loved Viken, but his tastes ran to large cities teeming with people and power politics. Public service was in his blood, and in mine as well. The entire family was expected to serve, although a Coalition fighter wasn't what he'd anticipated from me. Ours had been a tenuous relationship since I joined the Interstellar Fleet as a scout pilot. But that shock had worn off years ago.

He'd never truly forgiven me when Thalia followed in my footsteps and left Viken behind. That had been years ago. I'd thought long and hard about the decision to join the Fleet, and understood the risks. I survived. And although my father was reluctant to forgive, there had been a grudging respect in his eyes when we spoke. I was my own man, not a pawn to be moved on the family game board. I'd served Viken in a truer manner than people like my brother would ever understand. I'd served to fight for Viken, protecting it from an outside enemy too terrible to ignore. In joining the Fleet, I was keeping my family safe.

My father never saw it that way. He never would because unlike myself—and warriors like Rager and Liam—Dravon and my father had never seen the Hive firsthand. Never could grasp our enemy's true horror, the ugliness and evil of their true existence.

With Bella's arrival, my stance had become solidified. I believed in my family, loved them and their altruistic service. But I would continue to serve in my own way, with my own family. I believed in them. First.

Liam was no traitor. Bella had proven that. But now we faced a new problem, a bigger threat. My sister would not have acted alone. And though my heart was breaking for her, I knew her dissatisfaction had been festering for long months.

I was heart-sick, but not surprised. And that fact alone told me everything I needed to know. Now we needed to lure out the rest of the traitors. The IQC Array and surrounding station was critical to Viken's prosperity and safety. Nothing could put that at risk. Especially not my sister.

"I did, Father. And I haven't come here with a different stance. My family comes first. You preached that as a core command of our youth. I must have heard you say it a thousand times while I was growing up. And Bella is my family now. Bella, Liam and Rager."

"You are still a Tyrell," he countered. "This family must come first."

"Not anymore. You can either accept my family into the fold or not. They are my first priority."

"Then why are you here?" Dravon came into the room from one of the bedrooms, a petulant scowl on his face when he saw me. His nose looked fine, as if Rager had never broken it, no doubt thanks to a few minutes with a ReGen wand. But the narrowed gaze and clenched jaw was all the indication I needed that his opinions hadn't changed.

"Because he's my son. Show some respect." My father twisted in his chair to frown at my younger brother. "Or should I call Rager in here to break your nose again?"

"Thank you, Father." I bowed my head slightly out of respect. His support wasn't a hug, like Rager's father would have gladly given his son, but it was no less than what I'd expected. His honor was intact, it was part of the very fiber of his being.

Thalia's betrayal would hurt him the most.

"I am here to discuss a discovery Bella has made. She broke into our system, Commander." I changed my address here so he would know I was serious, and this was about more than just family. We were doing our jobs.

"Did she?" He leaned forward, clearly interested now that the uncomfortable discussion about family and loyalty was out of the way.

"Rather easily, sir. Took her less than four hours to have access to our entire planet-wide security network." I knew there was pride in my voice, but I didn't even try to hide it. My mate was brilliant and highly skilled. Watching her mind work had been fascinating and I admired her all the more for her intelligence and abilities. When she'd turned on me and informed me that she was not a soldier to be ordered around, my cock had been so hard I was about to explode in my pants like an untried youth. Gods, she was beautiful. I couldn't wait to claim her, to make her ours forever.

But first, I had to take care of Thalia and the VSS supporters who had infiltrated our station, who were helping her.

"And what did she find?" He was in full commander mode now, his tablet out so he could take notes, send orders over the communications network. Take action.

"Liam is innocent."

Dravon rolled his eyes. "Liam? Of course you would make that claim, big brother. But we all know he'll be executed," he said, walking over to sit across from our father.

I ground my teeth together as I stood between them, not wanting to get into an argument about that. There was a bigger issue. Thalia.

I took a deep breath, let it out.

"The true culprit has been discovered and identified. We have a full security feed of the traitor accessing the control panel and switching the security codes. And it wasn't Liam."

Acid churned in my stomach at what I was about to say. Thalia was my younger sister. Viken males were trained from birth to protect their female family members. I'd done that with Thalia, ensuring she was stationed near me so I could watch out for her, protect her, even though she was an adult.

Despite everything, she'd gone rogue, her actions turned from service to Viken to what? I couldn't understand why she'd chosen to betray us. I knew she was upset that Rager agreed to share a bride, but her infatuation with him had been little more than a young girl's crush.

My father would never forgive her. And while I chose Bella over my family, I was still a true Viken in my father's eyes. But Thalia? When he learned the truth? He would take the blow hard.

"Did your little *hacker* actually get through the security? You're sure she wasn't tricking you? It would be in her self-interests to make sure Liam was found innocent," Dravon said. While he made it sound derogatory, as if he was insulting her, I took it as a point of pride.

The corner of my mouth tipped up, remembering the flare of elation in her eyes, the way she almost vibrated with energy when she'd broken through the complex cyber defenses. I'd been so proud of her, so amazed that I'd fallen in love with her in that moment. But my joy had been like a bright flare, quickly extinguished when I saw the monitor, saw the traitor. The truth.

"She did."

When he didn't get the expected rise out of me, he slumped down in his chair.

My father was studying my expression, watching me closely. He knew me well, knew the worst was to come. "Well? You came to me for a reason. Tell me what you don't want to say."

The words were hard to speak. Words I never expected to utter. "I'm sorry, Father, but the traitor is Thalia."

Father stood, took a step toward me, outrage on his face. Perhaps he remembered all of the very private facts Bella had pulled up on him after just a few seconds, or perhaps he realized that I would never come to him with something like this if I had a shred of doubt. I loved my sister. Traitor or not, I loved her still.

"You're sure?" he asked.

As I nodded, Dravon stood. "You can't believe him! Thalia wouldn't do something like that. Stolen goods? Murder?"

"The monitors don't lie."

"No, but perhaps you do. Just how far would you go to save your friend Liam?" Dravon countered.

I glanced at my brother. People had thought we were twins when we were younger. We still looked much alike, but his unwavering beliefs hardened him. I recognized some of that in myself. It was a new discovery, brought about by Bella and her insightfulness. Somehow, over the course of one day, I'd softened around the edges. Yes, there was black-and-white, like seeing Thalia change the security codes for her VSS allies, but there was some gray, too. I had even let Bella take charge in bed.

I was going soft. But I still had to deal with my father. And Dravon.

"Thalia did it. You can put Liam before the hearing later, but the evidence will prove his innocence without doubt. And once that hearing is over, I will have to take a security team and arrest our sister."

"I want to see this proof!" Dravon said. He was becoming angrier; the idea of his sister being guilty brought out his ire. But was his belligerence fueled by anger or pride? Was he more concerned with our sister, or with the inevitable blow this would cause to the family name once he returned to the city?

"We will all see it at the hearing," Father said, his voice resigned, weaker than I'd ever heard it.

A beep came from my wrist unit, then Rager's voice. "Evon."

All of us looked to my wrist.

"Rager. I am with my family."

"Is Thalia with you?" he asked. He sounded...off. Why was he asking after Thalia when he was in the suite with Bella?

"No. She's not here. What's wrong?"

"Thalia. She stunned me. I...I refused her and she went insane. I tried to calm her, but the last thing I remember was her telling me she would ensure we would always be together."

I glanced at my father, then brother. Their eyes were wide, the truth coming not just from me, but from Rager, too.

"Are you hurt?"

"I was in the fucking shower when she hit me with current." He sighed, the sound loud through the speaker. "Still am. The water, shit, it made the ion charge worse. I can barely move."

"I'll call for a med unit," Dravon said, moving to the communicator on the wall. I stared at him for a moment, surprised he was so swift to help. He'd been so angry just a minute ago.

"Help is coming," I told Rager. "Wait. Where's Bella?"

"She's with you."

I stilled. "She's not with me. I took her to the suite to stay with you. I saw her go in."

"What?" Rager's voice changed then. I heard him stumbling about. "She never came in. I was in the shower and Thalia came in, came on to me. She was fucking naked, Evon."

I looked to my father, Dravon returning to our side. "The med team is on the way, Rager. And we all know my sister has wanted you for a long time."

"Yes, I know," Rager growled. "And I made it clear years ago the interest was not reciprocated. I have a mate now. I want Bella. Only Bella." His voice sounded weak, gravelly, as if he fought to remain conscious. I heard voices and sighed in relief as I heard a medical team enter the room.

My father spoke up, addressing the commotion. "This is Commander Tyrell. What is Rager's condition?"

"We've got him, Commander." A matter-of-fact voice came through the line, a female medical officer whose voice I recognized. "He's been stunned, but the ReGen readings are non-critical. He'll be back on his feet in a couple hours. Maybe less."

"Keep me informed."

"Yes, sir."

The communication went dead and I spun on my heel, heading for the door.

"Where do you think you're going?" my father asked.

"I have to find Bella." My mind was spinning, but the activity was welcome after the last hours of helpless waiting. I lifted my hand to the comm station in the wall. "Liam?"

In seconds, our system had tracked my friend. "Evon." Liam's voice sounded odd, restrained, as if we were strangers. Since we'd both had our cocks buried in our mate last night, and shared falling asleep in the same bed after, his cold demeanor startled me.

"What the fuck is going on, Liam? Where's Bella?"

Long seconds ticked by as tension flooded my back and chest, wrapping me up like a fist squeezing my entire body. "Liam? Fuck. Talk to me. Thalia's the traitor. I took Bella to our suite so I could meet with the commander, but Rager says he never saw her. Thalia offered herself to him in the shower, and when he refused her, she hit him with an ion pistol. She told him she was going to make sure they could be together forever. So, I'm going to ask you one more time, brother, where is our mate? Is she with you? Is she safe?"

Liam's sigh spoke volumes. "No. I left her with Warden Vora."

"What? Why was she at the testing center?" Cold terror and pain washed through me, nearly making my knees buckle. I pressed my forehead to the wall as I waited for Liam's answer.

"She requested a new match, Evon."

No. No. No. No...I didn't want to hear any more, but Liam continued, driving the stake deeper into my heart.

"She was convinced that you and Rager both betrayed us. She saw Rager with Thalia in the shower. After you refused to take her discovery to the panel immediately, she assumed you would do anything to protect Thalia, that you chose your sister over our family. She was hysterical."

I slammed my hand against the wall. This was my fault. I should have been gentler. I should have explained. But I'd done what I always do, take command and expect everyone to trust me.

With my sweet Bella, I realized, I hadn't yet earned that right. And now? Now, it might cost me everything.

I remained in place as my father called Warden Vora on his personal comm, but it was another who answered.

"Apologies, Commander, but Warden Vora is not here."

"Where is he?"

"He's been taken to medical. We are reviewing security footage now. He had a female in the processing center. A new bride. But she was taken hostage by the attacker."

I was breathing hard, every molecule of air burning through me like acid.

"Where are they now?" I yelled from across the room. On the other end of my comm, Liam's silence let me know that he, too, was listening.

"We don't know, sir."

"What do you mean, you don't know?" I demanded.

"The attacker was Lieutenant Thalia Tyrell. I'm sorry, sir."

"Stop fucking apologizing and tell me where she took Bella!" I walked toward my father as if I could strangle the young officer on the other end of the comm. "Where did they go?"

"We tracked them to the north exit."

"Fuck." Liam's shout came through loud and clear.

My father raised his hand, and since he was calmer than I was, I relented. "Pull up satellite tracking. We should be able to follow them across the tundra."

"Already working on it, sir."

My blood went from boil to steady simmer. Thalia had my mate out in the ice and snow. Why? What the hell was she going to do out there?

Nothing good. She'd already blasted Rager with an ion pistol, and she loved him to the point of obsession. I didn't want to think about what she might do to my mate. The one person who truly stood between her and Rager.

I was at the door when Dravon dashed across the room, grabbed his ion blaster and thigh holster. "I'm going with you."

I gave my brother a quick glance, not expecting anything from him, most of all support. "I'm going after Thalia. I will do anything to protect my mate. Anything," I repeated.

He glanced at my father, then his blue eyes met mine.

My father lifted his chin. "I understand. I'll be at central command looking at the satellite feeds and tracking data. I can guide you from there."

I nodded as he lowered his head and started barking orders. I had no idea why Draven had a change of heart, but now wasn't the time to figure it out.

"We have a hostage situation," I said. "Assemble a team of elites. We need to be outside."

Liam's voice echoed to me through the room. "North exit, Evon. I'll meet you there."

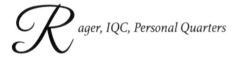

13

R ager, IQC, Personal Quarters

THE MED TECH WAS WAVING THE WAND OVER ME AS I PUT ON my clothes. I'd been stark naked when they'd found me in the shower as I talked with Evon. I had my balls hanging out for everyone to see and I didn't care. My mind was muddled from the hard shock Thalia had given me. My body was back to working again, enough for me to connect via comms to Evon. But with each pass of the ReGen wand, my muscles began to work, my mind began to clear.

As soon as I was able, I pushed off the tiled floor of the wet shower and made my way, albeit stumbling, to the wall unit and some clothes. When the med tech objected, I gave her a steely stare. "Follow along or stay behind."

I wasn't used to speaking so harshly, but Bella was out there. Not out in the IQC, but *outside*. With Thalia, who was fucking insane.

She'd scared the shit out of me when she'd called to me. I'd been under the hot spray, stroking my cock and thinking about eating Bella's pussy again when I heard her. I spun about, dick hard, and saw not the woman of my dreams, but Thalia. Naked.

She was gorgeous, all long limbs and perfect tits. But my cock had deflated at the sight of her. She wasn't the woman I wanted, the woman my body craved. Her dirty words had done nothing for me. When I'd told her to leave, told her that Bella was the only woman I wanted, ever, Thalia went crazy. Where she had the fucking ion rifle stashed, I couldn't remember, but the next thing I knew, I was all but sizzling on the shower floor as she loomed over me, hatred in her eyes. Her words chilled me, even under the hot spray.

"I'll take care of everything, Rager. Then we can be together forever."

She left me there, muscles in spasm, my spine and nervous system singed and struggling to function. Just what was she planning? How would she ensure we would be together, that nothing—no one—stood in the way?

That thought had me shoving my feet into my boots, grabbing my ion pistol and holster from the table. The med tech continued to follow me and wave the blue light over me. I felt better, hell, except for a headache, I was fine. Good enough.

"Enough." I'd fought the Hive in worse shape. I didn't give a shit about a damn headache, or any other injury. I was functional enough to walk, to go after my mate.

Grabbing the wand from her hands, I took a deep breath. "Thank you for your help. All of you." I looked to the other two medical officers who'd come to my aid but now stood to the side. "But I need to go. Now." I held up the wand. "I'll take this with me."

I didn't wait around to chat, but stalked out of the suite.

"Evon," I said, summoning him on my comms unit. I waved the damn blue wand over my torso and head as I walked because the hallway blurred a bit. "Location."

"North exit. Liam just arrived as well. We're here with Dravon."

I turned left down a corridor to meet them. Dravon was with Evon? That seemed insane, but *everything* was insane right now. I would question it later.

"I'm two minutes out."

"Too long," Liam said. "Meet us outside. Thalia has Bella out on the south plateau."

"My sister intends to kill our mate," Evon said.

My anger, usually easily quelled, roared to life. My head pounded, but I set the wand to the side of my skull, left it there, let the blue light do its work as I walked. If Evon was saying this, it was serious. I knew how intense and driven his family was. How he'd tried to be like them, but went his own way. He fought it daily, even up until the judicial hearing. I'd had to punch Dravon in the face for him. I'd do it again. Hell, I'd punch Thalia in the face, or worse, if she so much as gave my mate frostbite.

"That will not happen," I said. My voice was deep. Angry. So unlike me. I might be the patient one, but I had no patience in this moment, so I moved faster. Faster still. The deep rage, the berserker part of me, exploded from the depths of my soul with a silent roar. No one was going to take my mate from me. I'd tear Thalia's arms off before I let her get away with this.

"My father is feeding us coordinates," Evon added.

"I hear you, Rager," the Commander said, his voice surprisingly helpful. For once. "I see you on the positioning system. At the next corridor, turn left. Yes, good. As my son said, I'll guide you to them."

I wasn't sure if he was guiding me to Evon and Liam or to my mate and Thalia. Either way, I was going in the right direction. I healed myself as I ran toward the exit, I was going the right way. To my future. I just had to save it.

———

Bella

SHIT, IT WAS COLD. MY EYES HURT FROM THE GLARE, MY cheeks stung from the wind, but I was overheated marching along with Thalia at a ridiculous pace. The snow was thigh deep in places and barely covered the hard, rocky terrain in others. But Thalia pushed me on, prodding me with the end of her pistol when I stumbled. Threatening the lives of my mates if I refused to cooperate.

Sweat dripped down my back. I was no world-class athlete, but fury fueled me. And the constant nudge of Thalia's weapon in my back served as a nearly constant reminder of *why* I was mad. Why was she doing this? She and Rager were having their fun, playing their games. As much as it hurt me to admit, she'd already won.

"I was in the testing center requesting new mates," I said. I hoped my voice carried on the wind toward her. I wasn't going to look over my shoulder. I felt the damn weapon, I didn't need to see it, too.

My feet were heavy, the walking hard as we crossed

through the snow. It had been deep at first, near the main buildings, but the farther away we walked, it thinned out, became crusty as the terrain grew harsher. I wasn't trudging through snowdrifts any longer, but we were hiking rugged boulders and winding ice chasms. The wind must constantly pummel the land, hardening the frozen moisture to a crust that scrunched beneath our boots where the soft powder was exposed.

"I don't want Rager," I added. "I know you love him. You can have him, Thalia." That earned me a harsh nudge in my back. I winced.

"Liar," she countered.

"You said you weren't going to kill me. And you win. You can have him. I went to Warden Vora and requested to be reassigned, to have new mates. Just take me back. I'll be gone before dinner."

"You'll be gone soon. Somewhere Rager will never find you."

Shit. Was she just going to shoot and leave me out here for the wolves to eat? Did they have wolves here? Or polar bears? Or anything that would find me a tasty treat? "Why not just shoot me and be done with it?" It was a stupid thing, putting ideas in her head, but I wanted to know if I was going to be left out in the barren tundra to die.

"Oh, no. That would be too easy. I'm sending you somewhere. And you'll never come back."

I looked around. If she left me alone, I'd work my way back to IQC. I had a good sense of direction and it wasn't as if I could get lost. There was nothing to hide the rocky terrain, the snow. Yeah, it all looked the same and our footprints were most likely being blown away.

"Leaving me behind a rock isn't going to work."

She laughed then. "Leave you behind a rock? Gods, I thought you were really smart. I even liked you. Don't blow it now."

I glanced over my shoulder then, squinted. Her cheeks were red, her blonde hair blowing in the wind. And, yup, she had that ion thingy pointed at me. So much for all the helpful girly BFF chatting we'd done. While she'd been helping me pick out clothes, she'd been mentally backstabbing me. She must have been laughing that I knew nothing of her and Rager, but also jealous that he was fucking me, too.

I told her as much.

"Rager's mine," she growled. "Just knowing his cock had been in you, that his mouth has been on your pussy. Gods, that his hands touched you everywhere, makes me want to hurt you. He was supposed to be mine."

I spun about. She stopped in her tracks and I stared at her. Her face was lit by the sun and the snow. Her cheeks were red, her eyes wild, her hair blowing sideways away from her face.

"Supposed to be? Thalia, you were buck naked in the shower with him."

She grinned then. Not because we were friends, but because I was her enemy. "So you saw us, did you?" Then her smile fell away and a narrow gazed hatred took its place. "You saw him reject me. Tell me you were the only one he wanted."

I didn't see the hit coming. I'd been too stunned by her words to block the blow to the side of my head. I stumbled, fell to my knees.

"Fuck," I groaned. I'd been in fights before, cat fights really, with other women. Stupid drunken bar shit. But this?

This wasn't the same thing. She was armed and she was pissed and she'd just cold-cocked me in the side of my head with her pistol.

My entire head exploded with pain and my vision blurred. I tasted blood in my mouth and I was pretty sure my jaw was broken. And through it all I felt suddenly warm.

Rager had turned her away? They'd both been naked. She'd told him to give her his cock. But I'd run out. Missed the last. She wouldn't lie about Rager rejecting her. She had no reason to lie now. Not out here. If he'd fucked her, as I'd thought, she'd be gloating. Preening.

"Get up." She kicked me in the ribs with her boot and a sharp, stabbing pain had me crying out as I felt one of my ribs crack with a crunching sensation. "Keep moving."

She kicked me again and I grunted, but stood, holding one hand to my head. It pulsed and throbbed, but I ignored it as I began to tingle all over. Thank god for endorphins, or whatever this was, as my pain faded to a dull roar. Knowing Rager hadn't fucked her made me feel...better. But I was still confused. If he rejected her, why would he be helping her?

We walked another few minutes and she ordered me to stop moving. We were in the middle of nowhere, like North Pole nowhere. I couldn't run; there was no place to hide or avoid being shot. We were in the middle of a large flat area, the snow hard and flat in an unbroken plain beneath our feet. Looking out from here, it appeared to go on for miles and miles. An ocean of white.

I glanced over my shoulder when she stopped. She looked at her wrist communicator and slung a bag off her back, let it drop to the hard-packed snow. I hadn't even noticed she'd been carrying it. Of course, a big old space gun provided plenty of distraction. With a push of her boot to the back of my knee, she forced me to my knees.

I remained silent as I watched her set up some weird poles, metal bars, in a square around me. She placed her weapon on the ground beside her as she worked, but she was too far away for me to have any hope of taking it from her. It looked like she was putting up the corners of a tent... or a cage. I glanced around, shielded my eyes with my hands. I couldn't see the IQC anymore. I couldn't see anything but snow and dark, ragged rock. And machines, some kind of snow vehicle was moving toward us.

As I watched, I saw someone jump down from the vehicle and my heart thumped against my broken ribs. Hard. My heart pounded with hope as I watched them approach. I was being rescued. Thank god.

I shivered then. Adrenaline was making me feel weird. The sweat had stopped and now I was cold. So cold. I couldn't feel my hands or my feet. I tried to smile, but my lips didn't want to work. I thought that I should get up and run toward them, zig-zag around and let Thalia take her best shot. But the idea was like fog in my mind and my body refused to move.

"Incoming." The voice came from Thalia's communicator carried to me on the wind, and I frowned.

Thalia looked up from her kneeling position. Her heavy pants took the brunt of the cold from the ground, unlike my cream-colored ones. Yes, they were fur lined, but the fur wasn't thick, and even that wasn't doing much to keep the frigid air from me any longer.

Thalia stood, grabbing her weapon as she did so, waited as the two men—their size was a dead giveaway—to approach.

Oh. These weren't rescuers. These were her partners-in-crime. They wore heavy pants and boots like Thalia, their coats the color of their Sector, but heavy and coated in something shiny that, I assumed, blocked the wind. I couldn't see their eyes because they were shielded behind reflective glasses. Even their hair was covered by hats.

"You could have taken a rover, Thalia," one muttered. "No one will pay for a corpse."

What? Were they talking about me?

"She's fine. Trust me. The little bitch is tougher than she looks."

Holy shit. Yes, they were talking about me. They were selling me? Someone was going to pay them money for me?

Seeing the men in their thick coverings made me realize how cold the tips of my ears were, how my lips were going numb. I tucked my hands under my armpits, slumped my shoulders to curl in on myself, but nothing I did helped. I couldn't stop shaking.

"Stealing one would have been obvious. Tracking one even easier," Thalia countered. She shook her head as she eyed their vehicle. "Stupid. You should have walked."

"No one was supposed to be looking for us, Thalia. By the time we got word from you, it was too late to turn back."

"Fine. I don't want to argue. Let's do this and get the hell out of here. Help me finish setting this up."

It was obvious who was in charge. The two men took the metal pieces, put it together with remarkable ease. The one time I'd gone camping—I was a comfortable-bed-and-bathroom kind of camper—it had taken me an hour to figure out how to set up my tent and I'd somehow had an extra pole leftover.

When they stood back up, I took in what they'd made. I

blinked, looked again. It wasn't a tent. Why was I so focused on a tent? I was losing my mind. There were four poles at the four corners with weird black boxes on top. They were positioned about ten feet apart, in a square shape. Most of the time had been spent aligning them at perfect angles and securing their bases in the hard ground. Four poles. That was it. No nylon cover. No tent.

"Where's the tent?" I asked. I wanted to close my eyes, take a little nap. Whatever these guys planned, they weren't going to get much accomplished out here.

All three turned to me. They weren't shivering. They weren't huddled together for warmth. "Tent?" Thalia asked. She looked at her two cohorts with a shrug.

"We need to transport her before she freezes to death," the guy on her left said.

Was I freezing to death? I was cold, but dying? I just wanted to take a nap, not die.

Thalia strode over to me, grabbed my arm, and stared down at me with pure malice shining from her eyes. "You're going somewhere nice and warm. Lots and lots of sand. Sun."

I thought of the Caribbean. Palm trees. Fruity drinks with umbrellas. "Sounds nice," I replied, my teeth chattering.

"Nice?" I barely noticed a shrug of Thalia's shoulders beneath her heavy coat. "The raiders of Hobart 6 will think you're very nice. And the arms trade that will come from sending you there will be *nice* for me."

I frowned, my cheeks stinging from tightness. Sunburn? Windburn? Oh wait, tears. I had tears frozen on my cheeks. I lifted my hands to feel the frozen tracks, but my fingers were too numb to feel anything. "You're giving me to raiders?" I had no idea what a raider was, but it didn't sound good.

"I'm *trading* you," she clarified.

"Coordinates are set," one of the guards said, tablet in hand.

"Good. With you gone, Rager will be all mine. So will the weapons from Hobart 6."

She stepped away, the snow crunching beneath her boots as she left me in the center of the square.

"You're going to leave me here?" I asked.

She didn't walk far, just about ten feet away. "I'm not leaving you here." She pointed to the poles. "You're standing in the middle of a temporary transport pad. Goodbye, Bella."

My words stumbled out of the space between my lips, my cheeks and tongue felt numb. "I'm not going to...to wherever. I'm going to the testing center for new mates."

"Told you. She's not even wearing a coat," one of the men said. I couldn't tell who it was anymore.

"At least she's not fighting us much," the other said. "The cold's made her docile."

"Get her out of here," Thalia coaxed. "Rozin doesn't like to be kept waiting."

"You would know." The first man chuckled, but Thalia ignored him completely, her gaze locked on me as if she needed to watch me disappear with her own eyes.

Transport pad. Docile. Raiders. My brain was fuzzy, but I knew what they were going to do wasn't good. I didn't want to go to Hobart 1 or 4. Warm or not. I could be warm here with my mates. No, not Rager and Liam and Evon. With new mates. Big guys with warm bodies and a soft bed. Thick blankets.

No. Not Rager and Evon. They didn't want me.

But Rager hadn't been with Thalia. So maybe he did.

It all seemed too complicated. Really. All I wanted was my mates. I wanted them around me, making me feel safe, keeping me warm, holding me.

I wasn't going to let Thalia send me away. If I was going somewhere, it would be my choice.

"No way," I said, my tone adamant. I would have sounded like a bad-ass bitch if I'd been able to manage more than a whisper.

———

EVON

"I NEVER THOUGHT THESE THINGS WERE SLOW UNTIL NOW," I grumbled, at the wheel of one of the two rovers rolling over the rugged terrain.

Dravon was beside me, Liam and Rager in the seats behind. Liam's three-guard group was in the other rover, following behind. I'd been more than ready to run all the way to wherever the fuck Thalia had taken Bella, but Liam's good sense prevailed. Rager, usually the calm one, was too angry, too enraged to be much good. He'd fight like an Atlan beast, but not until it was time. For now, he sat, gripping the arms of his seat. I couldn't see him doing it, but I knew. I was as tightly leashed and my hands were practically strangling the steering controls.

"They walked. Father has confirmed that. We'll be upon them quicker this way." Dravon's words made sense and drove me on. "You're too emotionally invested in this."

I turned my head, looked at my younger brother. His gaze was out the window, squinting into the brightness.

"And you aren't?"

His blue eyes met mine for just a moment. "Your sister is a traitor. Your mate is at her mercy. I'd say you're worse off than me."

I grunted then. There wasn't anything else to say. It hurt learning our sister wasn't what we'd thought. *Who* we'd thought. But she wasn't a child anymore. Her decisions, her actions, were hers alone.

Pulling Bella into her twisted games? Sister or not, I would get my mate.

"There!" Liam pointed over my shoulder. In front of us we could see four people, although we were too far away to see exactly what they were doing. I wanted to go faster, but the rover was going max speed. My heart rate picked up the closer we got.

I knew the moment they heard us. They stilled, then two of them started moving about quickly. I could see now they wore the heavy coats and pants for outdoor exposure. One didn't. One all but blended into the snow. If it weren't for her dark hair, she would have been camouflaged completely.

"Bella's not wearing any gear," Rager said, his voice a rough growl. He'd slid up so he was positioned between me and Dravon.

"She's been out there how long, an hour?" Dravon asked, his voice betraying his nerves.

"Fuck." Liam's growl matched my thoughts exactly.

Bella had been outside, exposed to the elements in just heavy clothing for at least sixty minutes. She'd been walking, which helped, but she would still get cold no matter what. Life didn't survive here without protection in the harsh weather.

I shut down the rover directly in front of the group. I counted two guards, Thalia and Bella. The other rover circled around behind and two of our best marksmen climbed onto the roof of the vehicle. These traitors weren't going anywhere, not on foot.

Rager was out of the rover before I turned off the engine, the rest of us right on his heels.

"Bella!" he shouted, ripping off his coat as he ran to her.

She knelt on the ground and her shoulders were tucked in, her legs pressed together. Her hands were under her armpits and she was facing away from the wind. But she was in the middle of...oh no.

A portable transport pad. Thalia was going to send her somewhere.

"Stop," Thalia shouted, then fired her ion pistol at the ground, just in front of Rager. He held his coat in one hand as he stopped. He didn't turn to face my sister, just looked at Bella, and tossed her the coat.

Bella reached over to grab it, but fell to her side. Shit. She was as white as the snow, but her cheeks were bright red. So were her fingers. She was freezing to death before our eyes.

"Thalia, let her go," I said.

My sister didn't turn towards me, kept her eyes on Rager.

"She's going," she said. "She's going to Hobart 6."

"What?" Rager asked, spun to face Thalia, arms out. Liam's guards had their weapons out, pointed at the two Viken with Thalia. We were in a standoff, but Thalia still had all the power.

Hobart 6 was an outpost on the far side of the Atlan

solar system. Known for its raiders and militant pirates, it was no place for an unclaimed female. Based on what Thalia had been doing recently, she was sending my mate to those people as payment. Fuck.

"She'll be out of the way and we can be together," Thalia said.

Rager took a step toward her. Liam slowly moved in Bella's direction. He wasn't going to save her, he didn't dare with ion pistols pointed at her, just to block her from them. Dravon moved as well. They were big, big enough to form a wall. I stayed to the side to keep an eye on everything. I couldn't be laser focused on just Bella. Or just Thalia.

Where was the mobile transport control?

"She's my mate, Thalia. It's too late for that," Rager said. His words were like an ion blast. The truth had to be said, but it could set my sister off. It did.

"I *know* you don't want me. It's because she's here. With her gone, we can be together."

Rager shook his head, took a step toward Thalia. Her finger moved on the tablet in her hands.

"She's got the coordinates," Dravon said.

He was right. I could hear the humming from the pad now, feel the vibrations of it beneath my boots.

"Bella, get out of there," I called.

She turned her head to look at me. Her eyes were glassy, unfocused.

I stepped toward her. She was only twenty feet away. I could just pick her up and hold her. But that twenty feet...

One of Thalia's thugs shot in Bella's direction, which caused Liam's guard to shoot him. It happened so fast, the traitor was dead on the ground before I could blink.

Bella stilled.

"Stop!" I yelled. "Thalia, enough. You're surrounded. One of your men is dead."

"You won't kill me. I'm your sister." She whirled and faced me. In this moment, I didn't recognize her. Didn't recognize the little girl she'd been, the warrior she'd become. Her face was transformed by lines of anger and hatred, obsession and desperation.

"You're a traitor," Dravon replied. "You killed an innocent guard. Stole weapons and medical supplies for the VSS. You're sending Bella to Hobart 6, for what? A trade?"

"I'm not like you, Dravon. Not like Evon. She's going to Hobart 6. The deal's done." Thalia turned slowly and looked at Bella with pain in her eyes. "I'm your sister. You won't kill me. What would Father say?"

Her fingers flew then and I heard the familiar pre-transport buzzing. "No!" I shouted.

Everything happened at once. Liam leaped at Thalia to grab the tablet. I ran for the remaining thug with the blaster, stripped it from him. Rager went after Bella, but Dravon knocked him out of the way. Rager slammed into the ground as Dravon leapt to the pad. He lifted Bella and threw her out of the center of the transport area. The transport sizzle came and then he was gone.

"Dravon!" Thalia shouted.

Bella lay unmoving outside the transport area. Rager stumbled to his feet, ran to her. Liam's guard put the other traitor in restraints, Liam holding Thalia, taking her weapon from her, dropping it into the snow, then kicking it away.

Dravon was gone. He'd been transported instead of Bella. He'd protected her, saved her from whatever was waiting for her on Hobart 6. It wasn't good, but Dravon could handle it.

Thalia watched as Rager tended to Bella, scooped her up into his arms, tucked his coat about her.

"Rager!" Thalia shouted, her voice laced with desperation.

Rager met my gaze. I saw the harshness in it, all the while he was gentle with our mate. "She needs a ReGen pod."

His words were like ice in my veins. The ReGen wands could handle most injuries. But the full-body pods were for serious injury, could bring someone back from the brink of death. We only had a handful of the pods on Viken, and one of them was at IQC. Trembling with rage, not cold, I looked at the men who had climbed down from the top of the other rover. They were armed and deadly, which fit my current mood perfectly as I looked at my sister for the final time. "Get that traitor out of my sight. I never want to see her again."

Liam's guards dragged both Thalia and her man to one rover as Rager stalked to the other, climbing inside with Bella in his arms.

14

THE FIRST THING I HEARD WAS MY OWN BREATH ECHOING around me like I was wearing scuba gear, or had my head in a box.

Curious, I opened my eyes.

Not a box, a tube. I would have panicked, but the top was clear and I wasn't claustrophobic. Besides, the blue light all around me made everything tingle...in a good way. A warm, I'm-not-in-pain-anymore way.

I faded in and out, dozing like a sleepy kitten, so comfortable. I tried not to think about what waited for me on the outside. Rager. Evon and his family. Liam and his stoic pain.

All I'd wanted was to be loved, to have a family, someone who cared for me. But nothing had worked out and I'd hurt the men I loved more than I'd helped them.

Love. Yes. Dying in that cold, all I'd been able to think about was being with my men, surrounded by them, held by them, pleasured as they held me between them and took everything I had to give.

Faces appeared and disappeared and I blinked at them, confused. I felt like I was sleepy drunk, unable and unwilling to focus. Evon. His father. I heard some harshly whispered words and fought to pay attention, but the light was too warm and I was too tired to resist as it dragged me back under. Liam and Rager were here. All three of my mates' drifting by in a steady stream of worried, haggard faces.

Soon, I tried to say. Soon, I wouldn't be so sleepy. But no words came. Maybe I was dead. But they were here. I felt safe, and warm and surrounded by my mates. If this was heaven, it wasn't so bad...

———

Liam, Three Days Later

I paced our suite, the walls closing in on me as we waited for our mate to return from her time with Evon's father and others.

We'd all been banned from the meeting room, her mates excluded on the grounds of Coalition Fleet security. Which made every cell in my body rage. We weren't a danger to her; it was our job to protect her. There were no secrets between mates, but Evon's father seemed to think so.

Several battleship commanders had arrived yesterday, along with two council members from Prillon Prime, a shady bastard who identified himself as a member of the Interstellar Fleet's Intelligence Core, or I.C. He was a Prillon doctor named Mersan, and everything about him made my skin crawl.

Spies. Commanders. Politicians. And our mate had been stuck in a meeting with them for the last few hours.

"Sit down, Liam. You're making me want to break things." Rager sat in one of our chairs, his feet splayed wide in front of him, fingers interwoven over his chest, his head tilted all the way back so that his face pointed up to the ceiling. His eyes were closed, but I wasn't fooled. None of us were calm right now.

First Bella nearly died, and now this.

"What the fuck are they doing in there?" I demanded. "They've been at her for hours."

Evon leaned against the wall behind him, pretending to study his patrol schedules. "Finding out what we already know."

"And that is?" I asked.

"That Bella is extraordinary. And brilliant," Evon said.

"And dangerous." Rager added the last and I realized he was correct. Just a few hours and Bella had broken into the Interstellar Fleet's entire command structure, something that not even the Hive had been able to do. And the Interstellar Fleet? That wasn't just ICQ or even Viken. No, it was the military that included all the Coalition planets like Atlan, Prillon Prime and more. Hundreds more.

When the door opened unexpectedly, I turned to find our mate crossing the threshold. But she didn't look like our Bella, not anymore.

Rager stood.

Her long black hair was pulled back into a tight braid

and she no longer wore civilian clothing, but the uniform of a senior officer in the Coalition Fleet. Not a Viken uniform. No, our mate wore the camouflage marble of black, brown and gray that we'd all worn when we served on the battleship. It hugged every curve, and she had a weapon strapped to her hip.

Even Rager lost his cool as the door slid closed behind her.

"What the fuck, Bella?"

She smiled and twirled like a princess at a party showing off her new dress. "Is this cool or what? I'm a captain in the Coalition Fleet *and* a member of the Intelligence Core." Hands on hips, she grinned at all of us. "Now I can officially order all three of you around. On one condition, of course."

Evon rose, stalking her like prey.

Rager closed his eyes with a sigh and took three long, deep breaths. "Gods help us, why is she wearing an ion blaster?"

Me? I walked to her, took her face in my hands and kissed her because I could do nothing else. I didn't care if she was a captain or a cook, as long as she was ours.

"Bella, what are you talking about? What has happened?" Evon was beside me, but I wasn't letting go. I did move my attention from her lips to her neck, so she could answer him. I thought that was rather generous.

"What with my hacking skills and this new NPU they gave me, they want me to work with the Intelligence Core programmers to tighten our security so the Hive can't—" I hit a particularly sensitive spot behind her ear and she moaned before finishing her thought, "—hack into Coalition systems."

"What's the one condition, mate?" For a big man, Rager

moved like a shadow, and he was now on my right. "And why are you wearing a weapon?"

We had her trapped between us, her back to the door. But she wasn't protesting. No, she was clinging to me, her new weapon digging into my thigh.

"The weapon is a requirement. I am not to be taken alive."

We all let that one sink in and I realized just how important she had become to the planet, to the Fleet. Her abilities, in the wrong hands, could destroy worlds. If the Hive could break into the Coalition's control systems, they would kill billions. The war would be over and we'd lose. With Bella on our side, we stood a chance.

"We will guard you at all times," I insisted.

She lifted her brow. "Well, they left an entire squad of men here to guard me twenty-four/seven, so I don't think that's going to be an issue. They're bringing in more equipment too, and a few more programmers to work with me. They said Viken was deep enough in Coalition space that it would be a good I.C. Command center. And with the comms here at ICQ..."

"What?" Evon stepped behind her and opened the door with a wave of his hand. Sure enough, two unfamiliar warriors wearing Coalition armor stood at attention outside in the hallway. They nodded in salute, their shrewd, very serious gazes searching for Bella, confirming that she was unharmed.

With a nod, Evon closed the door and turned to her. "So, we'll have a bunch of uptight I.C. warriors stationed here to guard you. That's probably for the best, but what is this condition that must be met?" He wasn't arguing. Of the three of us, he was the highest-ranking officer and already worked in security. Evon knew exactly what was at stake.

Bella smiled and tilted her head back to expose her neck for my pleasure. "The condition, boys, is that I be officially claimed as soon as possible. They want to know that I'm committed to you, that I'm not going anywhere."

———

Evon

HER WORDS WERE LIKE A SHOT OF ELECTRIC CURRENT TO MY cock. Seeing her so happy, so full of fire, pleased me more than I'd thought possible. With Dravon back from his adventures on Hobart 6 and Thalia safely placed in a prison facility, the only thing that worried me now was her.

Bella.

My everything. This family was my entire existence, and I'd do anything to protect it. That the Coalition commanders and the leaders on Prillon Prime recognized my mate's abilities made me proud. But I took comfort in knowing she'd be guarded night and day, even when one of her mates wasn't with her.

I couldn't lose her again. I couldn't watch her body fight to survive in another ReGen pod. Thalia had broken my heart with her betrayal, but losing Bella would end me.

Liam was holding her, kissing her, and I had a violent urge to shove him away and take her myself.

But the harsh discipline that drove me needed to control that feeling, to redirect it. It was like fire in my bloodstream as my cock swelled to the point of pain.

"Do you know how to shoot that thing?" Rager asked. His hand reached for the weapon on her hip, but quickly moved to cup her round ass instead.

"Nope." She laughed and reached for him, burying her hands in his hair. "Will you teach me?"

"Of course." One touch, one smile, and Rager was tamed. I had to admit, I felt the same contentment I saw in his eyes, the same tenderness. The same lust.

Our mate owned us all—and Liam was having all the fun.

"Let her go." My voice held icy command and both Liam and Rager released her instantly, stepping away so we were all at equal distance. She knew who was in charge now, and her gaze found mine, a mixture of dread and desire in her eyes.

I never wanted to see the first emotion again. "You doubt my love for you?"

She studied me, shook her head.

After Thalia's mind fuck, I worried that she'd ruined us all. But having Bella almost freeze to death somehow gave us all clarity. It crystalized everything that was truly important.

I'd given her reason to doubt me once. I'd spend the rest of my life making up for that mistake.

Closing the distance, I knelt before her and lifted my face to gaze up into her eyes. I would not demand the answer I wanted from her. This had to be her choice. Because once she was ours, we were never going to let her go. "I love you, Bella. Do you choose us? Will you stay forever and accept our claim?"

"Yes."

———

Rager

THAT ONE WORD WAS LIKE THE CRACK OF A WHIP AND WE ALL moved at once. I removed the ion blaster from her hip as Liam pulled her uniform top off, exposing her soft skin and luscious breasts.

Evon was still on his knees, and he looked at me with pure mischief in his eyes as he pulled her pants down and buried his mouth at the juncture of her thighs.

"Bastard," I mumbled, even as Bella swayed on her feet. My mouth watered to take his place.

I caught her, holding her in place for Evon's attention as Liam removed her boots.

I expected Evon to stop, to pull back and take command, but it seemed my friend had discovered just how sweet our mate's pussy tasted on the tongue. Without Evon's iron control, this was going to be fast, a rising storm of passion and lust and need.

We hadn't touched Bella since we'd brought her to medical three days ago. She'd recovered in the ReGen pod, but she'd been tired and heartsick. Broken. So we'd cared for her, massaged her and fed her, made sure she always had a warm mate at her back and someone to hold her when she cried. Proven to her that we were the mates for her, that whatever she'd thought, the lies, were all wrong.

But now, it seemed our mate was fully healed—mind and body—and my cock jumped to attention as the sweet scent of her skin taunted me. Her lips were close. Her breasts round and full and pebbled into hard peaks. I took one in my hand and rolled her nipple as Evon lifted her leg, placing one of her knees over his shoulder so he could fuck her with his tongue.

Bella collapsed fully into my arms and I looked to Liam.

"Get what you need, Liam. This is happening now." I wasn't usually the one to issue commands, but I was too eager. My infamous patience didn't exist now.

Liam walked to the drawer where he kept the lube he'd need to make sure Bella was ready for him and I kissed her, hard and deep and with all the pent-up emotions of the last few days. I loved this woman. There was no other explanation for the painful joy that filled me when I held her in my arms.

Knowing I'd hear a protest from Evon, I ignored him and lifted Bella into my arms and carried her toward the bed. If he wanted her, he'd have to follow. Liam had stripped out of his clothes and stood waiting, cock hard. Evon did follow, without argument, and I heard his uniform hit the floor as well.

Bella wrapped her arms around me, her small hands playing with the hair at the nape of my neck as I waited for Evon to take his place.

We'd discussed this before, in the long hours spent deciding to send for a bride, to claim her together in the new kings' way. I knew her mouth was mine, as Liam knew her ass would take his cock and Evon would fuck her pussy. We'd fill her with our seed and watch her writhe and scream her pleasure as we all claimed her at once.

As I expected, Evon lay down with his back along the bottom edge of the mattress. His cock jutted up in welcome and his knees hung over the edge, his bare feet flat on the floor.

When he was ready, I settled our mate on his chest and she responded instantly, reaching up to claim his mouth in a kiss as she rubbed her wet, swollen folds over his cock. My cock ached to go there, but I knew her mouth would be just as perfect.

She didn't wait for permission, just lifted herself and lowered down over him, taking all of Evon in one quick slide. He groaned in relief and pleasure and I wanted that too. I moved to position myself by her head, her mouth in perfect alignment to take my needy cock.

———

BELLA

EVON'S COCK WAS HUGE, BUT I KNEW WHAT WAS COMING. More. I'd have Liam in my ass and Rager's hard length in my mouth. And I wanted them all now.

Right fucking now.

Maybe it was almost dying in the snow, or maybe it was my excitement at being able to do something amazing and challenging to help the Coalition Fleet, maybe I was just tired of being alone, tired of wondering if I was making the right choice.

Well, choice made. These men were mine, and I wasn't giving them up.

They'd been tender and sweet, caring and loving for the past few days. Days without them touching me in a sexual way. At first, I'd needed it. But the better I felt, the needier I became. I believed their words. I knew the truth. I was able to separate it from the lies and deceit that Thalia had woven.

Liam was free. Innocent. Rager had never wanted Thalia. She'd set him up just as she had me. And Evon? He hadn't been upset with me at discovering the truth, but with his sister. There was no longer anything between us. No secrets. And once I got Liam's and Rager's cocks in me, we'd be one.

These three were mine. All mine.

If another Thalia ever came along, she'd better hope I wasn't wearing my blaster.

I bounced on Evon's cock, grinned when he groaned under me, his eyes fluttering closed with pleasure. I felt like a wild woman, a complete rogue. I didn't recognize myself or the wildness coursing through me for my mates. Only for them.

My pussy was so wet, so eager for Evon. I was close to coming from his cock alone. I was used to the seed power now; his pre-cum seared through me, made me eager for my other two mates.

They thought they were claiming me, but they were wrong. Dead wrong.

I was claiming them. All three of them.

Pushing on Evon's chest, I sat up and ground down on his cock until my ass rested on his thighs. Then I shifted, rolling my hips to grind my clit against him.

So good. God, so damn good.

"Liam. I need you," I breathed. Yes, I felt empty without him playing with my ass, filling it. He'd made it so good for me the last time, I wanted more. I craved him there.

I didn't have long to wait. In seconds, his hard hand was on the back of my neck, pushing me down so my ass would be up in the air, right where he needed it.

A warm rush of liquid filled me there, then his finger, working the oil into me, making sure I was ready. It was so much tighter with Evon in my pussy. I'd have both holes filled. It was going to be so tight.

Evon pulled me down to his mouth and thrust his tongue deep as Liam aligned his cock with my body.

"Bella. Gods, Bella," Liam growled. "I love you."

"I love you, too." I reached behind me to grip his wrist where it rested on my hip. I squeezed and let go, so he'd know I meant it. His words made me hotter and my pussy clenched down on Evon's length like a fist. But that tightness was keeping my other mate out, so I opened up, relaxed as best I could, as he pushed forward, sliding into me, filling me more than I'd ever been before.

A whimper escaped me as I adjusted to their sizes, the stretch and burn more than I'd anticipated, but so powerful, so right.

I lifted my head and rested my forehead on Evon's so I could look into his ice-blue eyes, like twin flames. "I love you, Evon."

"I love you, mate."

They moved together, an orgasm building inside me as their pre-cum coated my inner walls. I clung to my control.

But I didn't want it like this. Not without Rager.

"Rager." All I did was turn my head and he was there, his huge cock swollen and ready, a drop of pre-cum glistening on the tip.

Now was the moment, but I needed to tell him how I felt. I'd been thinking about this for days as my mates pampered and fed me, held me and let me cry. They'd been my rocks, so patient and loving, they'd been more than I'd dared hope for. I loved them, all three of them, and they deserved to know that they'd won me over, heart and soul.

I looked up at him, just for a moment. "I love you, Rager."

"Bella, my love." He fisted his hand in my hair, his veins bulging from his temple as he watched my other two mates fuck me. "I love you, mate."

I smiled and swallowed him down, using one arm to brace myself and the other to work the base of his shaft as I sucked and swirled my tongue around his cock.

They all groaned when I did, moving together until I couldn't take any more. The seed power, their cocks, the pleasure they wrung from my body was too much.

I exploded into a million tiny pieces, but I let go, submitted myself body and soul, knew my mates would be there to catch me and put me back together. I was what held us together. I was what made us a family. And nothing would keep us apart.

A SPECIAL THANK YOU TO MY READERS...

Want more? I've got **hidden** bonus content on my web site *exclusively* for those on my <u>mailing list.</u>

If you are already on my email list, you don't need to do a thing! Simply scroll to the bottom of my newsletter emails and click on the *super-secret* link.

Not a member? What are you waiting for? In addition to ALL of my bonus content (great new stuff will be added regularly) you will be the first to hear about my newest release the second it hits the stores—AND you will get a free book as a special welcome gift.

Sign up now! http://freescifiromance.com

FIND YOUR INTERSTELLAR MATCH!

YOUR mate is out there. Take the test today and discover your perfect match. Are you ready for a sexy alien mate (or two)?

VOLUNTEER NOW!

interstellarbridesprogram.com

DO YOU LOVE AUDIOBOOKS?

Grace Goodwin's books are now available as audiobooks...everywhere.

LET'S TALK SPOILER ROOM!

Interested in joining my **Sci-Fi Squad**? Meet new like-minded sci-fi romance fanatics and chat with Grace! Get excerpts, cover reveals and sneak peeks before anyone else. Be part of a private Facebook group that shares pictures and fun news! Join here:

https://www.facebook.com/groups/scifisquad/

***

Want to talk about Grace Goodwin books with others? Join the **SPOILER ROOM** and spoil away! Your GG BFFs are waiting! (And so is Grace)

Join here:

https://www.facebook.com/groups/ggspoilerroom/

GET A FREE BOOK!

JOIN MY MAILING LIST TO BE THE FIRST TO KNOW OF NEW RELEASES, FREE BOOKS, SPECIAL PRICES AND OTHER AUTHOR GIVEAWAYS.

http://freescifiromance.com

ALSO BY GRACE GOODWIN

Mated to the Cyborgs

Cyborg Seduction

Her Cyborg Beast

Cyborg Fever

Rogue Cyborg

Cyborg's Secret Baby

Her Cyborg Warriors

Interstellar Brides® Program: The Virgins

The Alien's Mate

Claiming His Virgin

His Virgin Mate

His Virgin Bride

Interstellar Brides® Program: Ascension Saga

Ascension Saga, book 1

Ascension Saga, book 2

Ascension Saga, book 3

Trinity: Ascension Saga - Volume 1

Ascension Saga, book 4

Ascension Saga, book 5

Ascension Saga, book 6

Faith: Ascension Saga - Volume 2

Ascension Saga, book 7

Ascension Saga, book 8

Ascension Saga, book 9

Destiny: Ascension Saga - Volume 3

ABOUT GRACE

Grace Goodwin is a USA Today and international bestselling author of Sci-Fi and Paranormal romance with more than one million books sold. Grace's titles are available worldwide in multiple languages in ebook, print and audio formats. Two best friends, one left-brained, the other right-brained, make up the award-winning writing duo that is Grace Goodwin.

They are both mothers, escape room enthusiasts, avid readers and intrepid defenders of their preferred beverages. (There may or may not be an ongoing tea vs. coffee war occurring during their daily communications.) Grace loves to hear from readers!

All of Grace's books can be read as sexy, stand-alone adventures. But be careful, she likes her heroes hot and her love scenes hotter. You have been warned...

www.gracegoodwin.com
gracegoodwinauthor@gmail.com